THE WIFE OF A MEMPHIS HUSTLER

JAMMIE JAYE

The Wife Of A Memphis Hustler

Copyright © 2020 by Jammie Jaye

All rights reserved.

Published in the United States of America.

Published by Cole Hart Signature, LLC.

Mailing List

To stay up to date on new releases, plus get information on contests, sneak peeks, and more,

Go To The Website Below...

www.colehartsignature.com

TEXTING LIST

To stay up to date on new releases, plus get exclusive information on contests, sneak peeks, and more...

Text ColeHartSig to (855)231-5230

IN LOVING MEMORY OF JOSHUA DAVIS

ACKNOWLEDGMENTS

I wanted to take a moment to thank each and every person that has purchased one of my books, shared a post or even told someone about my books. You are the reason that I have made it this far. You believed in me. This book makes book number 18. Lord, I didn't think I would ever write this many books, but I have.

To my husband: Thanks for putting up with my loud typing and staying up late nights. You pushed me even when I didn't think that I needed it. I will forever be grateful for you. I love you so much. I know that I get on your nerves talking about characters that you know nothing about. You the real MVP.

To my kids: Lord knows I love you for listening to all of my rants when I was stuck and couldn't find my words. Thanks for all the late nights that yall stayed up with me while I worked on this book. Yall know first-hand how hard it was for me.

To my boo Ashley A.J. Davidson & Tina Marie Turner: I love yalllllllll so much. I will forever be grateful for all the late night FaceTimes. Yall are the only people that I know that will sit on Facetime with me for hours and not say a word. I met yall in this industry, but yall have become some of my closest friends. Yall dead ass are my sisters for life.

To Toyia Ann Hurst: Girl where do I start. You just don't know how happy I am to have you as my friend. You have been there for me through so much including listening to me talk about storylines all damn night. I love you Mz Toyia Ann.

To my readers: Thanks so much. Without you guys, none of this would be possible. Thanks for taking time out of your day to purchase my books. You guys are awesome, and greatly appreciated.

1

ALLIA

R ing Ring!!!!

My phone has been ringing all damn morning, and I had no idea who was calling back to back like that. I got pissed off after hitting ignore for the fifth time. I had just got in a few hours ago from work. I was off for the next two days, so I called myself putting my phone on vibrate so that I could get some rest, but that didn't work. I could still hear it vibrating. I worked at a hotel as a front desk receptionist as well as a supervisor at a community center. I rolled over and grabbed my phone, and it was my boyfriend Cell's sister, Gina. I rolled my eyes because I knew that she was probably calling to beg, that's all her ass did. I looked at the clock, and it was four in the morning. I also noticed that Cell wasn't home. Normally he always laid his jewelry on the dresser, and it wasn't there.

"Hello," I yelled into the phone.

"I've been calling you all morning you need to get to the hospital. Cell got shot," my boyfriend's sister yelled into the phone. When she said that I jumped up. I had to be sure that I heard her right.

"What did you just say?" I asked so that I could get clarification.

"He has been shot, and it's not looking good." I felt like my heart had fallen out of my chest. There was no way that what she was saying was true. What the fuck was he doing? I had been telling him for a while to watch who he was hanging around. Cell had been cutting hair in the same shop for the past three years that we had been together. Recently he changed shops and was running one for some guy that was from Atlanta. I didn't get why he would choose to do that because he was doing just fine where he was. It had been issue after issue ever since he started working for them, and now he was laying up in the hospital fighting for his life. I bet now his ass will listen to me.

I hung up the phone and grabbed the first thing that I could find then headed out the door. I knew that I looked a hot ass mess, but I didn't care. I jumped in my 2017 Altima that I had just gotten a few days ago and headed to see about my man. I made it to the Regional One Medical Center in no time. When I walked into the waiting room, it was packed. I spotted his mother and sister sitting in separate corners, I headed to check on his mom first. His mother got up and hugged me which was very out of character since she damn near hated my ass and the feeling was mutual. I could count how many times I had talked to her ass in the past year. In her eyes, I wasn't good enough for her son. She had made that clear plenty of times. I hugged her back though because I knew that she was going through right now. I made my way around the room speaking to the ones that I knew. When I made it back to his sister, she looked at me with sympathetic eyes.

"What are they saying? How is he doing, do we know what happened?" I asked. Just as she was getting ready to answer a girl walked in crying. Gina damn near ignored my ass and helped her sit down. I was lost as hell because I hadn't ever seen this girl before, and I had been around his family plenty of times.

"Gina please tell me that he is ok. I can't raise my baby alone," she cried. Why in the hell would she be asking Gina some shit like that? It must have been more than one person that got shot because I knew damn well that she wasn't pregnant by Cell. I looked at his best friend Ball, and he turned his head. I stood there for a minute because I knew damn well this girl was not saying what I thought she is saying.

"Gina there must have been multiple people shot because I know damn well that she's not talking about Cell." The whole room got quiet. The girl looked up and me like I was saying some shit that I didn't need to be saying. "Umm hello," I damn near yelled. I wanted answers.

"Look, that is none of my business. That's something that you will have to talk to him about," Gina said. I looked at that bitch like she had grown too damn heads. There was no way that she was serious. I looked at the girl to see if she was going to say anything. She gave me this look that I couldn't read. I got up to leave because there was no way that I was going to just sit here, and he had done this to me. At that point, his ass could have been dead for all I cared. This was the last damn straw I was done.

"Yea, you doing the right thing by leaving. I'm sure that he wouldn't want you here anyway," the girl spat. This was dead ass talking shit like I wouldn't beat her ass in this damn hospital.

"Don't do that Nia," Gina butted in. Now her big back ass wanted to speak up. She was fake as hell.

"First of all, girl who are you?" I asked. Lil mama just didn't know that she was fucking with the right one. I was with the shits.

"I'm his baby mama something that you will never be." I busted out laughing. Who in the whole fuck did this bitch think that she was talking to? She must not have checked my resume. I could have had a baby with that nigga years ago. I just knew better than to let his ass trap me. She was holding being his baby mama to a high standard like it was the best thing since sliced bread. What was really getting me was the fact that this girl was basic and young as hell. But if that's what he like then I loved it. I'm just happy that I dodged that bullet. I looked at his mother and saw pity in her eyes, and that was something that I didn't need. I had been through so much, and she never cared about my feelings before, so why in the fuck did she care now. The girl knew nothing about me, yet she was talking shit letting me know that he had been talking to her about me. I wanted to beat her ass for talking shit, but I knew that she wasn't worth me going to jail.

"Well, it looks like there is no need for me to be here. I will leave, but let me say this," I said looking to the baby mama then to his sister. "If you ever in yo life approach me again I will drag yo ass through this hospital. The only thing that saved you was the fact that I don't want to disrespect his mother and grandmother, but know the very next time that I lay eyes on you I'm going to show you how much of a bitch that I am. And just so you know I chose not to have a baby with his hoe ass," I told her before walking out the door. He had me fucked up. He better pray that he doesn't make it because if he does, I'm going to kill his ass. I was so fucking mad that I couldn't even cry. This was the last straw, hell, I was all cried out. I jumped in my car and pulled my phone out so that I could call my best friend, Erin. I called twice, and she didn't answer, so I knew that meant that she was on the phone with her sorry ass baby daddy. Just as I put my phone down a text came through from her.

Bestie: what's up boo I'm on the phone with Eli lying ass
Me: bitch you will never guess what just happened

Bestie: Oh lord what bitch

Me: so, I get a call saying that Cell got rushed to the hospital only to find out that the nigga got a whole fucking baby mama that he didn't think that I needed to know about. I'm so done this time.

I was reading over my texts and didn't realize that the light had turned red. I slammed straight into the back of the car that was in front of me. I just threw my head back before getting out the car. I guess it just wasn't my damn day. I knew that I had just fucked my shit up. Hell, I haven't had the damn car a week. I hadn't even paid my first fucking note.

I walked around so that I could see the damage that I had done. The car that I had hit was fucked up. When I notice the kind of car that it was, I just dropped my head. There was no way that I had ran into a fucking Maserati. Hell, that damn car was worth more than I made in a year. I was walking back to my car to get my phone when two niggas got out of the car.

"Damn,, Dub she fucked yo shit up," the nigga that got out of the passenger side joked as he looked at the car. I didn't see shit funny. But he wasn't lying I had fucked his shit up. I was jumping on the inside though because mines wasn't that bad.

"What the fuck you laughing at? There's nothing funny." I said rolling my eyes as I examined my car. I hate niggas that didn't know how to be serious. The younger one was still laughing, and that shit was pissing me off.

"Yo, lil mama watch yo mouth you the one that can't fucking drive," the one that I assume was Dub said. I rolled my eyes because I knew that I could drive. I just was distracted, but there was no way that I was going to tell his ass that.

"I can fucking drive. Here is my insurance information. Because that's the only way yo shit gone get fixed. So, if you think that you gone get some money out of me, you are mistaken. You probably slammed on brakes on purpose."

He just looked at me and started laughing. "Lil mama trust me I don't need yo money. I could buy you and yo car," Dub said. Just as I was getting ready to reply the police walked up. They had to have been in the area because I knew that I didn't call and by the looks of it neither did he.

The officer walked up and surveyed the damage and then turned to the driver. "Damn what's good Dub. Nigga, I ain't seen you in a while." Were they really sitting here having small talk? There was no way that this was really happening. I just walked towards my car and stood there. I looked at the time on my apple watch. I wanted to see how long they were going to sit here and talk. These niggas talked about everything from their parents to cars, but they had yet to talk about the two fucking cars that were here.

"Ma'am you can't leave the scene of an accident," the officer said as I was getting in my car. I couldn't do this right now. I just knew that my insurance was going to be high. Hell, it was high enough now since Cell was on it. With that thought, I made a mental note to take his ass off tomorrow.

"It's all good let her go so she can get her lil cheap ass car fixed," the driver said. That nigga had me fucked up. He had the right one on the right day. He was not going to stand here and talk about my car like it was a piece of shit.

"First off nigga, you got me fucked up. My shit ain't cheap. It may not cost as much as yours, but it ain't cheap. That's probably somebody else's shit that you are driving any fucking way. I hate broke ass niggas like you riding around in yo gal shit. Flossing like it yours." I got in my car before he had a chance to say something else. Soon as I pulled off, I gave my insurance company a call and told them what had happened. I was happy that they didn't ask me for a police report number. They just told me that someone would come by and take a look at it. The whole ride home I was thinking about the fact that Cell had fucked me over once again.

I made it home, it took no time because I was driving like a bat out of hell. I was so fucking angry that it was dangerous. If anything else happened, I would for sure go off the deep end. I had been through so much with him, and I knew that this would be the end. I damn near took care of this nigga when he fell off all because he had taken care of me when we first met. Back then he was the sweetest man that I had ever met but when money got low, all of that changed. Cell was one fine motherfucker. Women were always in his DM or on his jock just because. I had had so many run-ins with females over the years that it wasn't funny. I risked so much being with him.

I pulled up at the house and just sat in the car thinking about the day that I net his ass. We met a few days after my father had died. He picked me up when I was at my lowest, and we have been rocking ever since. He was even there for me when my grandmother died.

I got out the car and headed in the house so that I could pack this nigga's shit up. I thought about burning it all up, but that wouldn't do any good. That would just give his ass a reason to come the fuck back around me. I was also pissed at myself because I was taking bullshit from him like I was some ugly ass chick or something. I was 5'4 and 165 pounds with a nice round ass and some big ass hips to match. I was light skinned and had long black curly hair. A lot of people said that I looked like Dreka Gates in the face.

Just as I was walking in the door my phone rung and it was Erin.

"Hello," I answered. Bitch, are you ok? I'm finna come over there. I was just calling to see what you wanted to eat," she said into the phone.

"It doesn't matter whatever you get is fine."

"Ok, I'm on the way." That was what I loved about my boo,

she was always there when I needed her. Me and Erin met when we were in the fifth grade. Her mom and my aunt that helped raise me were best friends. Erin was the total opposite of me. She had the prettiest chocolate skin. She was around 5'2 and weighed no more than 145 pounds. She was stacked. She reminded me of Bernice Burgos.

I walked in the door and kicked my shoes off. It was kind of warm, so I opened the window to let some fresh air in. I wasn't ready to cut the air on yet, hell, my ass would be sick by the morning if I did. I walked in my room and looked at all of his shit laying around. That shit made me angry all over again. I went to the kitchen and grabbed the box of garbage bags that were sitting on the counter. I just started throwing shit in there. I didn't care if the shit broke or not. By the time that I was done with the first bag, I was neatly putting the shit in there. I was over this, and it was the last time that I was going to open my heart up to a nigga that wasn't worth my time.

2

———

DUB

"Yo shorty really just said fuck you," my brother Jabo said once I was done chopping it up with my nigga Jamal. I wanted to smack him for laughing and smack her fine ass for hitting my shit. Jamal and I used to rock hard when we were lil niggas, but when that nigga became twelve, I cut his ass off. I didn't fuck with the cops period. Once I was done talking to him, I headed to my cousin Grip's shop. Just as I was pulling up to his shop my phone rung. I saw that it was my nagging ass baby mama Roz. I just hit ignore and placed my phone in the cup holder. I didn't have time for her shit today. I knew for a fact that she didn't want shit but to get on my nerves. My baby was with my parents, so she had no reason to call me. Sometimes I wonder why in the hell did God make her ass my baby mama. She was by far the worst baby mama ever at this point. I stopped fucking with her because she wanted to do was party. She cared more about partying than she did about our daughter. I hate that she was like that because she wasn't a bad person. She just cared too much about hanging with her hoe ass friends. She couldn't see that they were using her.

"Mane, fuck that broke ass bitch. If Jamal wasn't standing

there, I would have smacked her ass," I lied as we got out the car. She was very disrespectful, and disrespect was something that I didn't tolerate. Truth is that shit did turn me on. I wasn't used to females acting like that. She was mad at me, and she hit my shit. That shit was crazy as hell. Then had the nerve to talk crazy.

"She was fine as hell though," Jabo said handing me the blunt that he had just lit. What he was saying was true, but I didn't say shit because if I had, he would have sworn that was the reason that I let what she did ride. One thing for sure was that if I had run into her somewhere else, I would have gotten her number. She was beyond fine and was beautiful.

"Fuck that bitch," was all that I said before walking in the door. Grip was sitting in the same damn spot that he was always in. That nigga didn't move from that damn spot unless it was time to go home or time to kill some damn body. All his ass did was sit in that damn chair and give out orders. I was trying to see how he made money.

"What the hell yall niggas doing back so damn soon yall just left," Grip said as we sat down.

"This nigga done let some bitch fuck his shit up and drive off," Jabo told him before pulling off the blunt.

"Nigga I hope yo ass is joking," Grip asked getting up walking out the door. He walked back in and a few minutes later looking mad as hell. He had just done this paint job a few weeks ago, so he was going to have to do the shit again. I don't get why he was mad he was getting paid.

"You let that bitch drive off? Was her shit fucked up? Nigga did she have insurance or something?" he asked. I just looked at him because he knew all of the answers. He just wanted to fuck with me.

I pulled my phone out and called my sister so that she could come and get us. I wasn't worried about my car. I had plenty of them.

My little sister Deaja was my heart. I made sure that no nigga would ever be able to win her with money. I was her big brother, so it was my job to make sure that she had everything that she needed. I don't know who spoiled her the most: me, Jabo, or my father. She could get anything from me as long as she graduate from college and open up her own business. I wanted her to have her own money so that when she found a man anything that he did would be a bonus. I knew that one day she was going to have to get in a relationship and I wanted to make sure that she was prepared. I had talks with her all the time so that she would know what to expect.

"Hey baby," I said kissing her on the cheek. Her car smelled so damn good. I had no idea what she used, but it always smelled good.

"What's good bucket head," Jabo said getting in the backseat of the car.

"Shut yo macho man head ass up. That's why Dub is my favorite brother," she joked. I knew that Jabo had to have thrown a middle finger at her because she licked her tongue out. They acted like big ass kids. I don't think there was a day that went by that they didn't argue. If you didn't know them, you would think that they were dead ass serious. The whole ride to Jabo's condo they went back and forth. I just pulled my phone out and scrolled through my texts. I had damn near twenty unread text messages. I was the king of not replying to people. Most times I forgot, and other times I just didn't care enough to reply. Most of the messages were from females

We all lived together for the most part. Jabo wasn't there much since he had a condo that he took all of his ho's to. He always had a new jump off. I was surprised that that nigga didn't have kids. He fucked way too many bitches. I told that nigga that one day his dick was going to fall off. Now don't think that I don't have as many bitches, because I do, I just don't fuck them all. I knew that shit was dangerous. Females get in their feelings, and that was some shit that I didn't have time for. Once I stopped fucking with Roz, I focused my time on my daughter and getting this money.

We made it home in no time. When we walked in the house, I headed to the shower because I had some shit that I needed to handle. Then I needed to go and get some pussy. I got out the shower and went to find something to throw on, just as I was walking in my closet my baby mama called again. I answered because that was the third time that she had called, so that meant that she wanted something.

"Yea," I answered.

"When is Jacey coming home? My cuzin is having a party for her daughter, and I wanted to take her," she explained. I knew that she had to want something. She was the best at showing off.

"I will call and ask. They went to the beach house the other day, so I'm not sure," I told her. I knew that she was going to get mad because I didn't tell her that Jacey was gone, but she would be ok.

"Ok Dub. Why didn't you tell me that she was gone?"

"I forgot." She just held the phone for a second before hanging up. I put my phone on the counter before brushing my teeth. Once I made sure that I was good and clean, I headed to get dressed. I settled on a Gucci sweat suit and some Jordan Katrina 3's. Once I was dressed and smelling good, I headed downstairs. My sister was on the couch with her ho ass friend Sam. I didn't fuck with that hoe. We fucked a few times, but I felt like she was just around my sister because of what she had. Sam was broke ass fuck. She was around here fucking niggas just to pay her cheap ass Metro PCS bill.

"Dae I'm gone. Make sure you keep yo company downstairs."

No one was allowed upstairs in my house, especially not Sam's ass. She was a snake, and I didn't want her ass walking around my house. She might get sticky fingers, and I would hate to have to kill her ass for stealing a pen or some shit.

I walked outside and stood there thinking about what car I wanted to drive. I decided on my Hell Cat. It was one of my favorite cars. I went to the garage and grabbed the keys. Soon as I sat in the car this female name Bri called. I sighed and answered.

"Yeah."

"That's really how you answer for me?" She asked like I didn't answer like this all of the time.

"What's up Bri?"

"I was calling to see if you were coming by," she said in a sad tone. She knew that she didn't have to call and ask me that. If I wanted to see her, I would have called and told her that. She probably had one of her friends over there and was trying to show off. That was something that she did often. She wanted everyone to know that she fucked with a nigga. Sometimes I thought that she really had in her head that we would be together one day. That shit will never happen though.

"Yea I'ma come there, but I gotta take care of some shit first," I told her.

"Ok baby I will be waiting for you," she assured me. We ended the call as I was getting on the e-way. Bri was cool as hell she just wasn't someone that I could see myself settling down with.

After riding for thirty more minutes, I pulled up at my warehouse so that I could do my daily count. I made sure that I came at random times to be sure that everything was good. My brother and I ran one of the largest drug empires there ever was in the state of Memphis. It was passed down to us from our father. We owned the city. There was nothing sold on these Memphis streets without coming through us first. We weren't like most niggas. I didn't have a whole lot of niggas working for me. I just had a few. I was the supplier. I didn't own any trap houses. I just made sure that the nigga that did own the trap house was always stocked up. The niggas that did work for me were close to me. Gram was my best friend and had been since we were in middle school. He was like a brother to Jabo and me. My family took him in after his mother got on drugs really bad. Then there as my cousin Suga, he was like the middle man. He handles all of the transactions for me. We had a few other dudes that were on the payroll that maintained the warehouse.

I was in the middle of my count when my phone rung. It was this female name, Toni. She had some of the best head that I had ever had, but her pussy was straight slaw. I answered on speaker since I was in the room alone.

"What's good baby?"

"Shit I was calling to see what's good with you it's been a few days since the last time that I heard from you."

"I've been busy ma. What's been good with you?"

"Shit really just school and work." That was another thing that I liked about her; she was smart as hell. I guess it's like that sometimes, you can't get everything in one package. We talked for a while longer, and I ended the call because my brother and my best friend Gram walked in.

"Nigga, who the fuck you on the phone caking with?" Jabo asked. That nigga was nosy as hell. I didn't answer because I knew that he was going to say something stupid. That's all that seemed to come out of his mouth. Jabo was a fool, he said whatever to whoever. He didn't care.

"What the fuck took yall niggas so damn long to get here?" I said changing the subject. I knew that if I didn't Gram was going to go off the deep end and I didn't have time for that shit. The two of them together was a disaster. They thought that everything was a joke. I couldn't get they ass to be serious for shit.

"I had to get me some pussy. I was fucking this big booty

bitch. Her breath was stank as hell, but she was fine. I just put some Carmex on my lip so that I would smell that shit." Gram said. I just shook my head that was all these two knew how to do. Fuck. Gram was just like Jabo when it came to females, he had one for every day of the week.

"That's nothing new. Yall shit gone fall off. I'm telling yall now don't call me trying to get me to do a drive by on a ho cause she done gave yall some shit that made yall dick fall off," was all I said before I started back counting.

"Did the nigga make it?" I asked Gram. The other day I had gotten word that this nigga that used to work with me was getting a little loose with his mouth. I didn't want the nigga dead because I want niggas to know what happened when you talked to damn much. I need that nigga to live to tell a mother-fucker not to play with me.

"Yep," Gram said as he rolled a blunt. I just nodded. I handed the money over to my brother so that he could count it as well. I headed to check the rest of the warehouse and make a few calls. Once I made sure that everything was good, I headed out so that I could get up with female name Bri. She didn't live far from where I was, so it took me no time to get there.

When I saw that there were cars out front that confirmed what I was thinking earlier about her trying to show off. I sat in the car and rolled me a blunt before getting out and heading in the house. I pulled my keys out and unlocked the door. When I walked in all conversation stopped. They all spoke to me as I walked through the house to the kitchen. By the time I came out if the kitchen they all were gone.

"Hey, baby, how was your day?" Bri asked as she walked to the back of the house.

"It was good. You didn't cook nothing," I asked as I looked through the fridge.

"Yo plate in the microwave," she assured me. I opened the microwave to see what she had cooked before heating it up. I smiled when I sent that she made my favorite, chicken, and noddle. Once I made sure that my food was warm, I dug straight in. It took me no time to finish because I was hungry as hell. After that, I headed to see what she was doing. I walked in the room, and she was laying in the bed ass naked. It was on from there.

3

JABO

It took me no time to do count. Once I was done, me and Gram both headed out. I needed to go and check on my girl. At least that's what I called her. I hadn't talked to her in a few days, and that wasn't normal. She's the only female that I hadn't fucked. We were like best friends, but she said that I couldn't call it that because she only had one best friend that she wouldn't let me meet. My brother and Gram didn't know about her because I knew they would clown my ass. I was hard on females and I knew that if they saw me being all soft and shit, they would never let that shit go. I pulled my phone out and called her.

"Hello," her sweet voice filled the receiver.

"What you are doing?" I asked.

"Finna go and check on my best friend. What's up?" she questioned.

"I was going to come and check on you."

"I will be back in a few hours or in the morning. She had a bad day, and I wanted to make sure she was good." We talked for a while longer until I pulled up at the female name Senna's house. When I pulled in the driveway, I saw that her mom's was

home and that alone made me pull off. Her mama was creepy
as hell. The way that she looked at me let me know that she
wanted the dick. What she didn't know was that I would fuck
her old ass. She was thick ass fuck. I sat there for a minute
debating on if I wanted to go in. I decide against it, so I pulled
off. As I was pulling off the street my phone rung and it was my
sister. I knew that she was finna ask for something. She was
spoiled as hell. "What yo Kermit looking ass want?" I answered.

"I was just calling to see what yo bobblehead ass was doing.
Don't come for me," she joked. She was my baby. "But naw I
was calling to ask could I go out with my friend and I'm not
talking about Sam. She works at the center that I volunteer at,"
she explained. I held the phone thinking about it. "I asked you
because I knew that Dub would say no. Please, Jabo I promise
that I won't get into any trouble," she whined. Deaja was nineteen and had grown up on us. She really didn't do much, but
when she was with Sam, there was always something going on.
"Sam's not going so you don't have to worry about nothing
happening." Sam was a hoe and there was no way that my
sister was going to be labeled as one.

"I need her name and birthday so that I can do a check on
her," I told her. People in the world were full of shit, and there
is no way that I would l allow something to happen to her. Hell,
we didn't have it like we do now when she met Sam otherwise
they wouldn't be friends.

"Ok I will text it to you," she happily said. That was all that I
wanted was for my baby to smile. I didn't care about shit else.
Just as I was pulling up at Gram's house, a text can through

Sis: Sh'Allia Williams 05/28/1998

I called Dub so that I could see if he was good with her going.
When he answered, he sounded like he was fucking so I hung
up. I didn't want to hear that shit I would just talk to him about

it later. I wanted some pussy but not enough to deal with these emotional ass females that I fucked with. When I walked into his house, I smelled food, so I knew that nigga was cooking. That's all that nigga did, and the shit was good as fuck, so I wasn't complaining. I was ready for him to take this shit to a new level. We had been trying to get him to open a restaurant for the longest, but he kept putting it off.

"Bitch you are not my girl. So don't ask me what the fuck I'm doing like I gotta answer to you. Fuck you think this is," he yelled into the phone. I just sat on the couch and rolled a blunt. I didn't have to tell him that I was here because he was alerted the moment that I pulled in his gate. That nigga house was like a damn prison.

After slamming his phone on the counter, he came and sat down and took the blunt from my hand. He looked like he was stressed. "Nigga, what the fuck is wrong with you?" I asked.

"Main this Tasha bitch always questioning me like she's my bitch. That shit be pissing a nigga off."

"You the one that made her ass feel comfortable enough to do that shit. My hoes know what up," I told him. He frowned up, and all I could do was laugh.

"Naw I just gave that her this good dick, and she wants it all to herself," he joked." I just shrugged my shoulders. Shit, I didn't know what that nigga had going on. Shit, I had my own bitches to worry about. We talked about the restaurant that he was about to open up while he finished cooking. I laughed on the inside every time I saw that nigga cook. He was a savage cook.

By the time that we were done eating Dub was walking in the door. That nigga looked like he was tired as hell. "Damn nigga that bitch must have sucked the life out of yo ass. You look tired as hell," I joked. He didn't reply; he just walked to the kitchen. I knew that he was going to fix him a plate.

Once he had his food, he came and sat on the other couch

and started eating. While he was eating, we passed the blunt around. This was our crew. We had other niggas that hung around us, but these were the two that I knew had a nigga's back no matter what. Gram had been around us for so long he was like a brother. There is no way that he would be addressed as a friend. Hell, even people in the streets thought that we were brothers. By the way, my name is Joshua Davis, and as you know, everyone calls me Jabo.

"What you wanted when you called?" Dub asked. That nigga killed that food in a matter of minutes. I guess he was really hungry.

"Daeja wants to go out with her friend. I have Band looking into her to make sure everything is good. I hadn't given her an answer yet. Once everything checks out, I will give her my answer."

"Why she didn't call me?"

"Cause nigga you would have said no," Gram added. He didn't reply because he knew that Gram was telling the truth. Dub didn't play when it came to her. In that nigga's eyes, she would never grow up.

It was getting late, so we all headed our separate ways. I need to get some sleep. I felt like I had been up and moving for the past few days. I had plans to go and look at this building that me and my brother planned on making a bar. I said my goodbyes and headed home.

When I walked into the house, Deaja was on the couch on her phone. I had no idea who she was talking to, but that had her ass smiling hard as hell. She noticed that I was looking and locked her phone. Whoever she was talking to had her blushing, and I didn't like that shit.

"Let me find out," was all I said before going to my room. Soon as I walked in, I headed straight to the shower. Once I was done I got my ass in bed. I just wanted to sleep.

4

———

ERIN

"I hope that you can get your car fixed," I told Allia. I had been at her house for a few hours. She was going through some shit and it was only right that I be by her side because I knew that she would do the same for me. We have been through so much together. Her ass was there for all my drama with my baby daddy. Just as that thought left my mind my phone rung. I saw that it was him calling and rolled my eyes. "What is it, Eli?" I answered. Eli was my sorry ass baby daddy. He has been in jail for the past three years. Before he went to jail, we were going strong, that is until I found out that he had three other kids. The crazy thing is he thought that I was just going to accept that shit. He had clearly lost his mind.

"Damn, I can't call my baby mama," he said as if that shit would impress me. I really wanted his ass to leave me alone. He had seven more years to be in there, and if he thought that I was going to stick around, then he was dumber than I thought. I was more than sure that one of his other baby mamas would love to hear from him. My baby Eliza was going on three and had never seen that nigga. When I first met Eli, I thought that he was a stand-up guy, but I was mistaken. He was a user. That nigga used me and then got ghost as soon as he found out that I was pregnant. He would call here and there, but that was about it. He didn't start calling until he found out that I was messing with this nigga from the hood. He was like any other nigga he didn't want me but didn't want anyone else to have me.

"No, you cant. Again I'm going to ask what do you want Eli?"

"Damn I was just checking on ya. You acting like you ain't my bitch or something. Every time I call, you act like I'm getting on yo nerves."

"I don't need you to check on me. I need you to check on Eliza. And I have told you before that I'm not your girl anymore." That was one of the problems that I had with Eli. He was more worried about me and what I was doing. Not one time did that nigga call and ask about his daughter. The only reason that he had been calling so much was because one of his lame ass friends saw me out.

"Bye Eli," I said hanging up. I was over his ass I blocked the number that he was calling from. Hell, he better be glad that I'm not low down I would call the warden and tell him that the nigga was calling me from a cell phone.

I was getting irritated because he was intruding on my time with my bestie. She was going through some shit, and she needed me so what he was talking about didn't matter.

"Girl why you doing that main like that?" Allia asked as if I was going to answer. She was my best friend, so she knew what was up. I was sitting on the bed in Allia's room while she cleaned up. There was something different about her. She was way too calm. Normally she would have been mad, but it was like she didn't care. I knew then that she was done. It had been a week since Cell was shot and she hadn't said shit about that nigga. She had taken all of his shit to his mama house and everything. Hell, I just knew that she was going to be fucked up, but she seemed to be good.

"So are we still going out?" I asked as I scrolled through Instagram.

"Hell yes, bitch we in there. I'm finna go pop this pussy for a real nigga."

"Girl I'm not finna play with yo ass. You done lost yo damn mind. But for real I wish that Eli would just leave me alone girl. I'm over his ass," I told her. She just laughed. I knew that she wanted to say something, but she kept it to herself. She didn't like his ass, but for some reason, I loved that nigga at one point. It was probably because he was my first. We had a bond until he broke it. The day that he did that I knew that I needed to let go. He was pulling me down, and I couldn't have that.

"Ummm," was all that she said. I laid back thinking about what I would wear. She told me that she was bringing someone else I just hoped that she wasn't full of shit. You how hoes can be.

"You talked to Cell?" I asked just to see what she would say.

"Hell naw fuck that nigga. I'm done and that's on my mama. He done really fucked up. That bitch can have him. And thinking back to that day, girl how about insurance say that they not gon pay for my shit because I don't got a police report. I was mad as hell." Just as I was getting ready to reply someone knocked on the door. She got up and opened it. It was a sheriff. He handed her a paper and walked off. She opened it, and tears started rolling down her face. It was like she was stuck because she wasn't saying anything.

"Allia what's that?" I asked. She just handed it to me and walked off. I read the paper and followed her in the room.

"Can you believe that nigga hasn't been paying the rent. It's two fucking months behind that's over two thousand dollars that I don't really fucking have," she said plopping down on the bed. I knew that she didn't have money like that but I did. I made a mental note to go and pay it for her. I knew that if I tried to give it to her she wouldn't take it and there is no way that I'm going let her get put out. My dad was well off; he was a retired doctor. My parents were old as hell when they had me. I was twenty-one, and they were in their sixties plus I was an only child. They had my baby so damn spoiled. When I first got pregnant, I just knew that they would be mad, but they were happy as hell

"Don't worry boo. It will all work out. So tell me about this car," I said trying to change the subject. I didn't want her to be crying about some shit that could be taken care of with a phone call. She knew that I was going to make sure that she was good. There was no question about that.

"Girl it's gone cost me twelve hundred dollars to get it fixed my ass gone be riding around like that until I save up some more money. Shit, I gotta spend what I got paying my damn rent. Cause I'm not finna let this shit go on my credit hell I just got my shit back on track. One thing that I do know is that every day I find a new reason not to ever take that nigga back." I could tell that she was serious. One thing I will say was that she was good when it came to paying bills. So I knew this was messing with her.

"Shit that's how it was with Eli. I thought that I could be a down chick, but that shit is not for me. He has been gone three damn years my shit got cobwebs. I want some dick ASAP. I can't wait to find a nigga to stick dick all in me. My pussy gets wet when a fine nigga walks past me. Shit, I damn near fucked the pizza guy the other day," I explained. She knew that I was dead ass serious. The closest I had been to a man was my friend, and there was no way that I would fuck him.

"Bitch you stupid ass fuck," Allia told me as she handed me a drink. She thinks that I'm playing, but I'm dead ass serious. That pizza man was fine as hell. My ass been ordering pizza from they ass ever since. I don't really be wanting that shit I be waiting to see his fine ass so I can play with my pussy.

"I'ma be straight up with whatever nigga I find. I'ma be like

"Look baby boy, I just want some dick. I'm not trying to be yo boo or no shit like that I just need a nut. I'm sure that you do too so it's an even swap," she was laughing so hard that she damn near choked on the water that she was drinking. Truth is the only man that I wanted, I knew that I could have he was a straight up hoe. There was no way that I was going to put myself out there like that.

"So you telling me that you just gone fuck a nigga just like that. I can't do this with today." I laughed

"Well bitch it is what it is," I told her as I scrolled on my phone. We talk for a while longer about what we were going to wear to the club. Although it was a few days away, we still need to get in our mind what we were going to wear if not we would be going anywhere.

The NEXT DAY

I woke up with a major fucking headache for some reason. I rolled over, and the bed was empty, so I knew that Allia was probably gone to work. I headed to the guest bathroom so that I could shower. I was off today, so I was going to go to my parents' house and spend some time with them and my baby girl. Once I was dressed, I headed out. I made sure that I set the alarm and locked the door before going to my car. My phone vibrated just as I was starting the car. I saw that it was my friend dude. I didn't feel like talking, so I hit ignore. I had to do that to him some times because he acted like I was his girl and not his friend. I liked him, but he was too much of a hoe for me. So I made sure that I kept his ass in the friend zone.

It took no time for me to get to my parent's house since they didn't live far from Allia. As I pulled in my parent's driveway, my dad was walking out of the house. Eliza was following behind him as always. When she laid eyes on me, she took off running. I could do anything but laugh. She was so chubby, and her little legs were moving so fast.

"Hey mommy's baby," I greeted her as I picked her up.

"Me and papa going to get ice cream," she told me with so much excitement that it caused me to laugh. I just smiled. I loved my happy baby. She was my everything, she was all that I needed. Since they were headed out, I decided that I would go with them so that I could spend some time with them. My mother walked out of the house just as we were getting in the car. Once we were all in the car, my dad pulled off. My baby talked the whole way to the ice cream shop. She had just started at a new school, so she had so much to tell me. We made it in no time. Eliza was so excited that she damn near jumped over me getting out the car. She was so damn pretty. She was the spitting image of Eli ass. That was one of the good things that he had done.

"What you over here thinking about baby girl?" my dad asked as he handed me a chocolate cone. I loved chocolate ice cream.

"Nothing just life dad. I want so much more. I want love like what you and mom have. I just have to come to grips with the fact that I will never have that. I'm in love with a man that won't even be with me and me only," I cried. I don't know what came over me. My dad was my diary. I could talk to him about anything.

"Baby girl if that man wants you he will show you. Don't put your life on hold waiting on him. Move on. If it's meant to be then it will be," he schooled me. My dad was my go-to. He was way more understanding than my mom. Now don't get me wrong I can go to my mom for anything, but my dad was just more open. I knew that what he was saying was right, but I also knew that I just couldn't let that love go.

After we finished with ice cream, we headed back to their house. Just as we were pulling in the driveway my phone rung.

It was my friend calling back again. This time I decide to answer because I knew that he wasn't going to stop calling.

"Hello."

"I have been calling yo ass all day. I was about to come and find yo ass," he said making me laugh. See he was doing that shit again, acting like I was his girl.

"Maybe I didn't answer because I was busy," I teased. I knew that was going to make his ass mad. He swore that I was never supposed to be too busy for him unless I was doing something for Eliza.

"Play if you want to. I was calling to see what you had planned, I wanted you to go and look at this building with me," he explained. He was in the process of opening a bar. He had been telling me about it for a while. Hell, in my eyes he had enough going on. He and his brother owned a club as well as a cleaning company, a car lot and studio. Honestly, he was every-thing thing that a woman would want. He was fine and paid. He was just the biggest hoe in the city.

"I can do that. I'm at my parent's house spending time with my baby. What time you want me to meet you?" I asked.

"I will pick you up from yo parent's house in an hour," was all he said before hanging up. He knew that I didn't want his ass coming here. That would have my mama asking all kinds of questions. I could feel my dad looking at me. He was sitting in his favorite chair. I looked over at him, and he was smiling.

"What you smiling for old man?"

"Nothing I was just looking at my baby," he assured me. I was an only child, so my parents took pride in me. That was one of the reasons that I went so hard at everything because I wanted to make them proud. I sat and talked to my dad until I got a text from Jabo saying that he was outside. I was happy that my dad was in the bathroom because I knew that he would have followed me and I didn't have time for that. Just as I was getting up, I heard the doorbell. I just rolled my eyes because he knew what he was doing. By the time I made it to the door my mom already had opened it.

"Good afternoon is Erin home," he asked in the sweetest voice. I had to make sure that it was his ass at the door. Jabo was by far the rudest damn nigga that I had ever meet, and now he was sitting here being sweet and shit.

"Yes she is handsome please come in," my mom offered. I just rolled my eyes because I knew that she was about to be extra. When he came in the door, he walked right past my ass like he came for her. They were just talking. I knew that my dad would be coming in here soon as he heard Jabo's voice. I just stood at the doorway and watched him charm my mother.

"Who was that at the door," my father asked coming from the back of the house.

"Erin invited her friend over," my mom said. I did not invite his ass over here. I told him to come and get me not come and sweet attack my mama and shit. My father came further in the room and looked at Jabo then he looked at me.

"Dad this is Joshua. Joshua this is my father Dr. Allen Turner," I said introducing them. Jabo stood up and walked up to shake my father's hand. I just knew that he was going to do him how he did Eli. I just stood there waiting for shit to go left.

"How are you Dr. Turner," Jabo said shocking the hell out of me. This was not the nigga that I knew. The nigga that I knew was mean and rude to every damn body. They shook hands, and a smile graced my father's face. I knew right then that my father liked his ass.

"I'm great Joshua. Let's go to my man cave and have a talk. Baby why don't you get Joshua some lemonade," he instructed my mother. She got up and did what he asked. I knew then that I would never be able to get rid of his ass.

It seemed like they were down there forever. I kept peeking down the stairs hoping that I could hear at least a little of their conversation. I knew how he was, but I also know how my father was. I wanted them to like each other. I wanted to be with Jabo one day, but I knew if my father didn't like him that wasn't going to happen.

"Girl get over here," my mom fussed. I sighed and walked to the table where she was sitting.

"I just need dad to like him."

"He will baby," she assured me. My nerves were bad, so I went to get Eliza down for her nap. I need to calm down. By the time that I was done my father and Jabo were in the kitchen talking to my mom. When I walked in, they all looked at me and stopped talking, letting me know that they were talking about me.

"Why yall looking at me?" I asked. No one said anything which caused me to have an attitude, I just walked out of the room. I few minutes after Jabo came in the living room with my parents following behind him.

"You ready?" he asked me. I just nodded and got up. When I made it by the door, my father came and hugged me. My mom was just standing back looking. I loved my parents so much. I couldn't have asked for better ones. Once we said our goodbyes, we headed to the car so that we could make it to his appointment on time.

DEAJA

A FEW DAYS LATER

"Deaja yo friend at the gate," Dub yelled through the intercom. I was doing this paper that was due next week. I liked to stay ahead of my work that way I won't get behind. I didn't need to hear my parents or my brother's mouth. I closed my laptop, grabbed my phone and headed downstairs. I had to chill with her in the living room because Dub didn't allow her to walk through the house. He said that she was a thief, but I didn't think she was. Once I made it downstairs, I hit the button to open the gate for her.

"I thought you had a paper due?" he questioned.

"I do."

"Well, why would you call company over?" This is what I hated about living with him. He asked a million damn questions. But I knew that my father would ask more, so I didn't complain.

"I didn't invite her over Dub. I haven't even talked to her today," I explained. He just nodded and walked off. I walked to the door so that I could open it for her because I was more than sure that his mean ass locked it just because he knew that she was coming.

"Hey boo," she greeted me soon as she walked in the door. She had so food in her hand, so I knew that mean that she wanted to gossip. We both sat on the couch and opened the bags that she brought with her. The smell of A&R Barbecue hit my nose I swear my stomach rumbled.

"So what been up," I asked.

"Shit really girl just working. Yo brother must not be here," she asked. That was weird because she never asked me that. It was like lately she hadn't been herself, and that was bothering me. Hell, she was even dressing differently.

"Yea," was my reply. She was looking around, and that alerted me. She had been in the same damn room plenty of times so why was she looking around like something new was in here.

"Girl how about I saw yo sister-n-law last night at the strip club," she told me. I just looked at her because I didn't fuck with Roz so why was she telling me anything about her. I wasn't with the talking behind people back shit. If I wanted to say some shit about you, then I would just tell yo ass. Roz knew how I felt about her, so there was no need for me to talk about her. It was like slowly I was getting annoyed when I was around Sam. She was so extra, and I didn't have time for that.

"That's good." I guess she could tell that I didn't want to hear that so she moved on and started telling me about some girl that Jabo was messing with. After she ran her mouth for a few more minutes, she got a phone call and rushed to leave which I was happy about.

Once she was gone, I got dressed so that I could go to the community center. That was the only place that my brother let me go to in the hood. I love going there, that's where I met Allia. She was the sweetest, and kind of like the big sister that I never had. She was the only person that I could talk to about anything. I knew that she would never tell anyone or judge me.

"Dub," I yelled through the house so that I could see where he was at. When I heard his voice coming from his office, I headed that way.

"I'm finna go to the community center,' I told him. He was looking at something on his computer, so he didn't look at me right away.

"Hold on I will drop you off and pick you up," he assured me. I knew that was coming he never let me drive, but Jabo did. Jabo let me do way more than Dub did. That's why when I wanted to do something I always ask Jabo because Dub was going to say no without even listening.

"Ok." Since I knew that he was doing something I just headed to the kitchen to fix me something to drink. I pulled out my phone and got on Instagram. The first picture that popped up was my brother's fine ass best friend Gram. That man was so damn fine, but I knew that he would never look at me that way. I liked the picture and kept scrolling. By the time that I was tired of scrolling Dub was walking in telling me that he was ready to go. I grabbed my purse, and we headed out. The whole ride he was on his phone.

"When mama coming back from Florida?" I asked just to strike up a conversation. It was too damn quiet for me. He ass was always in his own world.

"I think they come back in two weeks. You know mama get out there and don't want to come home." He wasn't lying. That was my mama's favorite place they went there at least five times a year. Hell, I was surprised she hadn't moved there. She always said that she wanted a house on the beach in Florida, so that's what my father got her.

"Aw ok, I want to go to Mexico," I told him. That was one place that I hadn't been yet. Every year we went on a family trip. I was hoping that telling him that would make him choose

Mexico. The rest of the ride we made small talk. He dropped me off and told me to call when I was ready to get picked up.

When I walked into the gym, Allia was standing near her office. She looked so sad. If you didn't know her, you wouldn't be able to tell, but I knew because I knew her. She smiled when she saw me walking over as she always did, I gave her a hug and then went to sit my things down in her office.

"What's on yo mind suga?" I asked sitting down in the chair that was close to where she was standing.

"Girl so damn much. Hell, I didn't know where to start," she mumbled.

"Let's start with Cell because I'm sure that he has something to do with it," I urged. She just looked at me. I knew that she didn't expect me to say that, but I knew that he was the cause of her pain as always.

"So he has a baby on the way. I found that out after he got shot. He just has changed. Now I'm not saying that he was the best man ever, but the nigga was ok for the most part. Hell, now I didn't know his ass. Everything has changed from the way he talks to the way that he dresses. It's like he is trying to be someone else," she said. I could tell that she was trying to keep herself from crying.

"Ok, so what else?"

"Then girl I ran in to the back of some fine ass nigga's car. I fucked his shit up," she laughed. I could help but to join in because she was laughing so damn hard.

"What the hell girl. How the hell did you do that?" I questioned.

"On the damn phone. Hell, I was just happy that I didn't fuck my shit up too bad," she admitted. I was happy that she was laughing because lord knows that I couldn't take her crying. We sat near her office and talked until the last kids were gone. Then I called Jabo to come and get me since I wanted to talk to him about going out. I wanted to take them to my brother's club, but I knew that I couldn't tell Jabo that. I was just going to go. Once I was there, he would be able to tell me that I had to leave. When he pulled up, he had Gram's fine ass in the car with him. I slid in the back seat behind Jabo so that I could have a good view of Gram. I had the biggest crush on him, but I knew we could never be together.

SAM

I needed to find a way to get back close to Daeja. Lately, I had been distant because I didn't want her to know the kind of shit that I was into. I hated that my cousin moved here ever since he touched down I've been miserable.

"So what did you find out?" my cousin Corry asked me soon as I walked in the door. His ass didn't even give me time to sit down before questioning me. I just kept walking because he was going to let me get undressed and settled before he started asking a million questions. I knew that he was going to be mad, but I didn't care; he would be ok.

When I walked into my room, my boyfriend Slim was laying in the bed looking at TV. I was not expecting that. He usually was in the streets all damn day, but just my damn luck, not today. I met Slim a few months ago when I was at the club. When he approached me, I thought that he was a broke nigga, but boy was I mistaken. Now he didn't have money like Dub and Jabo, but he was paid. He made sure I was good, and my bills were paid, and that was enough for me.

"Hey baby," I spoke as I undressed.

"What's up I was waiting for you to get home so that you

could take care of daddy," he flirted. That was one of the things that I hated about Slim. He was older, much older so he was always saying some shit like that and that shit creeped me out. I just kept moving as if I didn't hear his ass. Damn, he don't give me time to want to give his old ass no pussy because he always asking. Hell, I thought because he was old, he wouldn't want to fuck but that's all he wanted to do.

"Let me shower baby," I insisted.

"Ok." He got off the bed and walked over to where I was. He grabbed my face so damn hard I was sure that he had broken my damn jaw. "Let me find out you out here fucking another nigga you gone wish that you never met me. I already wished that shit. Now hurry up and come and suck my dick," he gritted. That was another thing he had a problem with and that was keeping his hands to his self.

"I'm not," I managed to get out. He then kissed me on the jaw before walking back to the bed and laying back down.

Soon as I closed the bathroom door, I broke down. I had gotten myself in some shit that I couldn't get out of. I was about to cross the only person that cared about me outside of my family. I felt so stupid because I had let my jealousy get the best of me.

I decided to just take my time in the shower because I was dreading sucking his dick. He had gray hairs on his dick, and that was so nasty to me. Once I was done cleaning myself, I walked out of the room. He was lying naked. I turned around and grabbed a towel so that I could roll my eyes without him seeing me.

When I turned back around, he was stroking his dick. After I was on the bed, I wrapped my mouth around his gray ass dick and closed my eyes. I needed to think about someone other than his ass. It seems as if I was becoming a damn sex slave. I made him nut as fast as I could so that he could get out and go get in the streets like always. I got up from the bed and went to brush my teeth. I hated the taste of his nut; it was salty as hell.

"So did you find out anything?" he asked.

"Naw they were home so I knew that if I started asking questions, they would hear me. I think I'll try and take her to lunch to see if I can get some answers. Hell Corry should be getting the info he's the one that she's damn near in love with." I looked up at him and knew then that I had let my mouth write a check my ass couldn't cash. His hand went across my face so fast that I didn't have time to brace myself, so I fell off the bed.

"Watch yo fucking mouth and find out something that I can use to get to them niggas," he gritted. I just nodded my head. I couldn't talk because my mouth was full of blood. He left the room, and I ran to the bathroom to wash my mouth out. I needed to find a way to get out of this relationship, or my ass was going to be dead.

I sat in my bed thinking of how I could get some information out of Daeja. She was private, and I knew that she would never tell me anything about her brothers. I picked up my phone to call the one person that I knew could help me. I made the call then headed to see if Corry was still here. As I was walking down the stairs, I could hear the two of them talking.

"So you think that she not trying to find out shit?" Corry asked.

"Hell naw you know that's her friend. Females don't know what they want. You need to get her to meet up with you. From what I have heard she them nigga's heart. So if we have their heart, then they will fold," Slim explained. When I agreed to this, they promised me that Daeja wouldn't get hurt.

"You know that Sam is going to go crazy if we hurt her," Corry said.

"She will be ok. I need to get out of here and go see what up with Cell. I know he holding something back," Slim said walking off. I just went back to the room. I didn't want to talk to either of them. Corry lied to me and told me that he really cared about her. Now I know that it was all lies. I needed to think of a way to warn her without telling her. I can't lie and say that I wasn't jealous of her, but I cared. I didn't want them to hurt her.

7

ERIN

A WEEK LATER

S hit with me a Jabo had been weird as hell since the day that he met my parents. It was like he was doing anything to make me happy. Like before he left he gave me three thousand dollars to go shopping. I was going to turn it down, but I decided that I would just take my bestie out and get her a few things. I knew that she wasn't going to want me to do it, but it she deserved it. Allia was by far the sweetest damn person that I knew.

"Ma," I yelled as I walked through my parent's house. I knew they were probably outside with Eliza. She ran they house. Whatever she wanted she got when she was over here. That's why she always wanted to be here. I made my way to the back of the house. Just as I thought they were on the back porch.

"Hey baby girl," my mother greeted me. I hugged her and then picked up my baby. She was giggling so hard that I could help but to laugh. She was so damn goofy.

"Look, mommy," she said showing me the picture that she

was drawing. My baby loved to draw. I can't tell you how many times I had to repaint the walls because she decided that she was going to draw on them.

"I love it, baby," I assured her. I kissed her and sat her back where she was. I took a seat next to my mom. She was reading on her kindle as always. I grabbed the slice of cake that she was eating on and eat some.

"Where is dad?"

"He went to play pool." That was one of my father's many hobbies. I sat and talked with her until Allia called. Soon as my phone started ringing, I walked into the house.

"What's up bestie. You off work?" I asked praying that she was.

"Yep just walked in the house. I called to tell you that Cell baby mama followed me on snap. Now I should be petty, but I don't got time," she sassed. Allia was a better person than me because I would be posting all kind of shit to make her ass mad.

"You better than me bitch. But look I'm finna come get you I need you to go somewhere with me. I'm at mama's house, so I will be there in like twenty minutes," I told her. I knew that she was going to try and object, so I hung up.

"I'm gone ma."

"Ok baby be careful," she told me. I grabbed a slice of cake and headed to Allia's house. On the way there I called Jabo to see what he was doing. I was kind of missing him; I just wasn't going to tell him that.

"What's good baby," he answered.

"Nothing headed to go and get my bestie and then going to the mall courtesy of my *friend*. I held the phone because I wanted to hear what his reply was going to be. I knew that he was going to say something crazy.

"Oh, so that's what I am to you," he scowled.

"I mean what am I to you?" I asked. I wanted to know what

he felt for me, and this was the perfect time to find out. I been wanting to ask but I didn't want to get my feelings hurt.

"You mines just know that." I was shocked because I knew nothing about that. Hell, I thought that we were just friends. I can't lie though I was smiling big as hell.

"I guess."

"Yo Erin stop playing with me. Call me when you get to the mall. Don't make me have to call you Erin." I was smiling so damn hard because since he had met my parents, he had been showing out, but I loved it. I was enjoying watching the man that he was becoming. He made sure that I was good at all times no matter what.

I used my key to get in the house. She was sitting on the couch eating some chips. "Let's go," was all I said before walking back out the door. Once she was in the car, I headed to the mall. She was so in her phone that she wasn't paying attention to where I was going. When we stopped, she looked up. "What we doing here?" she asked.

"Shopping ain't that what you do at the mall," I said getting out of the car. She slowly got out. I could tell that she was finna start fussing.

"Erin girl I don't got no damn money," she fussed. I just kept walking. That was why I didn't tell her to meet me because I knew that she would have pulled that. I headed straight to her favorite store. She was the only person I knew that loved Macy's. We shopped for damn near three hours. We finally were ready to check out when I felt someone walk up behind me and rub my ass. I turned around ready to click the fuck out, but soon as I laid eyes on Jabo's fine ass, I smiled.

"I was finna smack yo ass," I laughed. He kissed me, and I swear the whole world stopped. That was the first time that we had kissed. He looked in my eyes, and it was like at that moment I fell in love. I know that sounded cliché, but it was the way that I felt. We both just stood there for a second and looked at each other.

"Damn can yall get a room," Allia joked. "Bitch what did I miss because as far I knew you didn't have a boyfriend but here you are in the middle of the mall locking lips and shit. Damn fill a bitch in," she said causing Jabo to look at her. Soon as he looked at her, he started laughing.

"Yall know each other?" I asked. She was frowned up, and he was laughing like someone had said a joke. The guy that was with him was looking just like I was.

"Yo this the one that fucked Dub's car up," he told his friend. The guy looked at Allia and giggled. Hell, I wanted to know what was so damn funny.

"What's funny about that," I ask Jabo. He stopped laughing fast as hell. He grabbed me and pulled me closer to him. That shit gave me butterflies.

"She is the first female that ever punked my brother," Jabo said kissing me on the neck.

"Oh, shit baby this is my bestie Allia, Al this is —."

"Her future husband Joshua but you can call me Jabo," Jabo finished my sentence. "Aw and this my bro Gram," he added.

"I didn't punk him," Allia said with an attitude. At that moment it hit me that it was his brother's car that she had hit. I had a real blonde moment. Jabo paid for all of the stuff that we had on the counter, and we headed to the food court. We all decided on the Chinese place, so we got in line. Jabo was all over my ass. I guess he called himself marking his territory. Everyone that walked up to him he introduced me as his girl. I guess he just made the decision for me because we said that we were going with the flow.

Just as we were ordering our food, a girl walked up and stood next to us. I knew that she was one of his many hoes. He was so into kissing all on my neck and shit that he didn't see her.

"So this is why I can't get you to answer the phone," she damn near screamed making everyone look at us. Jabo raised his head and looked at her. He didn't reply he just started back hugging me from behind.

"Damn baby you smell good," he told me causing me to blush. He didn't see a need to reply, so there was no reason for me to say anything. I looked at Allia, and she was looking at ole girl ready to attack.

"So you gone act like you don't hear me Jabo," ole girl yelled this time. Jabo pulled away from me and looked at her. I knew by the look on his face that he was getting ready to say some fucked up shit.

"Yo get on with that can't you see that I'm with my girl," he calmly stated.

"So, you was just all in my shit and now you in here hugged up with this hoe embarrassing me," she said causing Gram and Jabo to laugh. That was my time to jump in because she had me fucked up.

"Embarrassing you. Fool you out here making a scene about a nigga that only call you when he wanna fuck. You want to know why I'm not answering because I don't need yo dry ass pussy or your slaw ass head. You a freak hoe. I told you plenty of times that you could never be my girl. Now I'm going to say this one time and one time only. Don't ever disrespect my girl again," He said as he grabbed my hand and we all walked off. I guess that wasn't enough because she came behind us still talking shit. Just as I was about to turn around he grabbed me and kissed me causing her rant to stop. "She's not worth it baby. You got what she wished she could have," he whispered in my ear. I smiled and walked off. He was right; she didn't deserve my energy.

8

———

ALLIA

I was dying laughing at how ole girl just cut up in that damn mall. That was crazy. I was proud of Erin though because she was known to beat a bitch's ass. When we got outside, we decided that we would all chill. I just prayed that Jabo didn't tell his brother that I was around. I didn't have time for his ass. I had enough going on right now. Since Erin wanted to get in the car with Jabo, I drove her car, and Gram was in his own car. I had no idea where we were going I was just following them. My mind drifted off to Jabo's fine ass brother. I knew that he was bad news by the way that he carried himself.

My phone rung as we were driving. I saw that it was Cell and I debated on if I wanted to answer or not. I really didn't have shit to say to his ass, but a part of me wanted to hear his explanation.

"What?" I answered.

"Yo you really put me out?" he asked as if he didn't know the answer. Cell couldn't have been that damn dumb to think that I wouldn't put his shot out.

"Cell, why are you calling me?"

"Damn so I can't call you now. A nigga laid up in the

hospital and I done seen everybody but you. What's up with that shit?" This nigga had lost his damn mind. They had to have given his ass something that made him delusional. Cell was so used to me always taking his cheating ass back, but that wasn't going to happen this time. He had cheated but had never gotten anyone pregnant that I knew of. I loved Cell, but I need to love myself more. I was damn near homeless because of this nigga, and he was calling asking me if I put his shit out. I should have told his ass that I got put out just to see what he would say. After all the shit that he had done, he still thought that I should be there for him. Hell, I can't remember the last time his ass was there for me. I remember when my grand-mother died. She was all that I had. I didn't know my parents, so she was the one that raised me. When she died, he didn't come home for three days because he said that he didn't have time to hear me crying. 'That shit was soft' is what he told me. I needed him. I felt like my world was over, but he wanted to be in the streets.

"Cell, please leave me alone," I urged. I wanted him to just disappear out of my life because he was toxic. I just seem to keep going backward. I needed to move on, and so did he.

"Baby you not gone let me explain. Look Allia I was drunk one night and fucked her because I was mad at you. A few months later she came to a nigga talking about she was preg-nant. She trapped me, baby," he lied. I could hear it in his tone. I knew that his ass was lying. I knew him better than he knew himself.

"Cell, you lying. I know that and so do you. I took so much shit, and I'm done this was it for me. I love you, but I need to love me more. Cell we are done," I told him before ending the call. I didn't realize that I was crying until we pulled up to a huge ass house. I followed them in the gate. Once I saw them getting out, I got out. When we walked in the house, I was taken aback because it was so damn nice.

"Yall make yall self at home. I'm going to whip up something to eat really quick," Gram said before walking off. Jabo and Erin were all hugged up, and my bestie looked so happy. It had been years since I saw her ass smile like that. I was just happy that she was open to getting to know someone because Eli took her down through there. Hell if he and Cell didn't hate each other, I would think they were brothers, with they cheating asses.

"He can cook?" I asked Jabo. He just nodded.

"Can you please not tell your brother that you know me. Cause I cannot pay for his car. Hell, I can't pay for my own," I admitted.

"That nigga ain't worried, I think he had his eye on you though," he told me which caused me to roll my eyes.

"I'm good on that. I just got out of some shit, and I don't need them problems," I sassed. I was good on a nigga. I couldn't take any more heartbreak. Cell had taken care of that.

"Naw you just wasn't fucking with a real nigga baby girl. My nigga, he a real one. Let me call him up so he can come over and show you, Gram yelled from the kitchen. I jumped up fast as hell going to stop him. When I walked in the kitchen, that nigga was cutting up onions. I just rolled my eyes and walked off. I need to get away before they called his ass for real.

"Erin I'm just going to take your car and go home because these niggas not finna get me caught up," I told her as I picked up my purse.

She looked like she was disappointed, but she just let me leave. On the ride home I kept thinking about how I was going to get Cell out of my life. I just wish that I had my granny so that she could help me through this. I need to know what to do, and I knew that she was the only one that would have been able to help me. I made it home in no time. Once I got to the house, I went straight to the bathroom. I need to soak in the tub so that I could get my mind right. I was doing my best to make it seem like I was ok, but I wasn't I was hurt. I had given him the best years of my life just for him to go and get someone else pregnant. Part of me wondered if I was the cause of that. Maybe I worked too much. I was working two jobs and going to school. In my eyes, I was doing that for us. I guess he didn't see it that way.

I undressed and stepped into the hot water. I submerged my whole body. The water helped me relax. I needed to get my life in order. I wanted to get back in school, and I wanted to save so that I could open my own community center. I love kids. I also wanted to open a home for teen mothers. There was so much that I wanted to do and I would be able to do that with him in my life. I wasn't looking for love, but I knew there was someone out there that could love me and push me to make my dreams come true. I sat in the tub until my skin got wrinkled. I got out then headed to bed. I had work in the morning, so I wanted to get some rest.

9

JABO

Erin had a nigga's nose wide open. After talking with her dad and hearing what the last nigga had done to her, I wanted to show her what a real nigga was. She was the first female that I actually wanted to be seen with. I was happy to call her mines. She was everything a nigga could want. She was beautiful smart and thick ass fuck. I had been trying to get to this point with her for so long. Now that I was here there was no going back. I was going to make her my wife one day. I just need to get all of my hoeing out the way. I couldn't wait to tell my mom because I knew that she would be happy. She had been telling me for the past year that it was time for me to slow down and find me a woman, but that was the last thing that I was thinking about.

"Y'all ran my friend away," Erin joked.

"We were just playing. If it's meant for them to meet again, they will sooner or later," I told her. I could smell whatever Gram was cooking, and that shit smelled good as hell.

"So we a couple now?" Erin quizzed. I looked at her like she was crazy because I thought that was something that was already understood.

"What kind of question is that. I thought that was under-stood, baby."

She smiled big as hell. That was all that I wanted. I just wanted to make her happy the way that she made me happy. I kissed her and could have sworn that I heard a small moan come out of her mouth. I pulled back and looked at her.

"What you looking at me like that for?" she asked. I just shook my head. I grabbed the remote and powered the TV on. We found a movie to watch while we waited. When we were halfway through the movie Dub walked in the house.

"Damn why I didn't get an invite to the party. Shit, I thought I was coming over to get a nap and yall over here having a party and shit," Dub said as he sat on the other couch. He looked at Erin and nodded his head. That was his way of telling me good pick.

"So yall really gone silently talk about me as if I'm slow and don't know what yall doing?" Erin laughed. I knew she was going to catch on because she was observant as hell.

"What you talking about baby?" I asked. "Yo, Dub this is my baby Erin. Erin baby this is my big brother Dub."

She looked at him and then nodded. After that, she picked up her phone. I knew that she was texting her friend. "I wish that my girl was here so we could talk about yall in silence, so yall know how it feels."

"Who is yo friend? Dub asked. Soon as he said that Gram walked out of the kitchen and stood there. I guess he wanted to see his face too. I rubbed my hand down my face because I was trying to keep from laughing. Dub was looking at me because he knew that I was trying to keep from laughing.

"So you remember the girl that ran into the back of your car?" I coached. I knew then he would think about who I was talking about.

"What about her?" he cautioned. I could see the wheels in

his head rolling. I knew that his ass was going to put two and two together, that's why I didn't reply back.

"Yo that's her friend," he guessed. I nodded my head, and that nigga's face was priceless.

"Small world, huh," Gram hinted. Dub just looked at him. I was dying on the inside. Erin shrugged her shoulders and laughed. I knew that he was going to be on Erin's ass about them meeting now.

"Where is the bathroom?' Erin asked. I pointed to the hallway and then she got up. Soon as we heard the bathroom door closed. We all looked at each other and busted out laughing.

"She going in there to call her friend and give her the whole run down," Gram said before going back in the kitchen. Ten minutes later she walked in back in the living room. She was smiling big as hell. I wanted to say something, but I decided to let her be great.

"Yall can eat," Gram advised. We all damn near ran in the kitchen. He made some chicken fajitas. There were all kinds of toppings. Erin was so focused on eating that she didn't see that I had put a cup of Kool-Aid in front of her.

"Damn nigga, have you been feeding her?" Dub asked making her look up. My baby did not play when it came to her food. Her little ass could eat.

"Shut up nigga. This shit is too good to be talking," she said with a mouth full of food. For the rest of the day, we all just sat around and chilled.

It was getting late, so I headed to take Erin to go and get her car. When we pulled up to her friends' house, she kissed me and got out of the car. I watched her as she walked to the door. When I saw her walk in, I pulled off and headed to the house. On the ride home, I thought about the fact that I hadn't checked out the girl that Deaja wanted to kick it with. I pulled my phone out and pulled up text that she had sent with the girl's information. I looked at the name and laughed. There couldn't be too many people with that name.

Me: what is Allia's real name: Wifey: Sha'Allia…..why

Me: just asking
Me: you can go, but don't make me regret it
Sis: Thank you I love you so much

Knowing that Allia was Erin's friend I didn't get her checked because I knew that she was good. Deaja was gone be happy as hell. I just smiled because I knew that I had made her day. An hour later I pulled up at home. I walked in the door, and Daeja was on the couch knocked out. I grabbed a blanket and laid it over her before heading to my room. When I laid down my mind went straight to my baby, so I decided that I would Face-time her.

"Didn't you just leave her," Allia answered.

"Aye, let me go get my brother real quick." I joked. I laid the phone down like I was going somewhere. She handed the phone to Erin soon as my face left the screen. When I saw Erin's face, I picked the phone back up.

"Don't be doing her like that," Erin laughed. I knew that would get her ass off the phone fast.

"She started with me. What you doing? I miss you," I admitted.

"Nothing finna head home."

"Ok I will meet you there," I told her making her smile. I knew that I had been with her all day but I was missing her and I also wanted to wake up to her. We said our goodbyes, and I got up to pack me a bag. I needed to have some things at her house anyway. Once I was done, I headed to her house.

10
———

DAEJA

THE NEXT WEEK

I was happy that my brother said that I could go with Allia. They don't let me do much, but being here with them was better than being there with my parents. My parents wouldn't let my ass do shit. They didn't play at all. I also knew that Jabo would say yes, whereas Dub would say no before I had a chance to get my words out good. He was worse than my father some times. He was fun to be around, but when it came to my protection, he didn't play. I was happy that Jabo didn't ask where we were going because I would have hated to have to lie to him. There was no way that he would have said yes. I held my phone hoping that he wouldn't text back. When he didn't after ten minutes, I headed to my room so that I could call Allia.

She hadn't really met my brothers because I wanted to make sure that she was really my friend not just trying to be around me to get closer to my brothers like Sam did. Sam thought that I didn't know that was the reason why she was around me. She was looking for a come up and she thought that I was going to be that for her, but she was mistaken.

"Hey boo," Allia answered.

"He said that I could go friend," I sang into the phone with so much excitement that I'm sure she was laughing. She swore that I was extra as she would call it.

"Girl ima need them to let you be great." I had told her how my brothers were, I just never told her anything else about them.

"So look, me and my bestie are going to dinner before the party you should meet us so that yall can officially meet. I know that yall will click because we clicked. I can come and get you if would like," she stated.

"I will just drive," I assured her. Her coming to my house was a no go. I wasn't ready for her to meet either of my brothers yet. Sam was the last person that I had let come over and ever since she had been coming when she wanted to, and I didn't need that from Allia.

"Ok cool well let's meet at Houston's on Poplar around two," she instructed. As we were talking my boyfriend texted me causing me to block out what she was saying.

Him: u sleep: Me: Naw talking to my homegirl what up baby

"Girl I know you hear me. That nigga must be texting you?" she asked getting my attention. Allia was the only one that I told about my boyfriend. I wanted to tell my brothers, but they would have a heart attack. They didn't want me dating at all. If it were up to them, my ass would be alone for the rest of my life. My boo Corry was all that I wanted. He was handsome and smart. I met him at school. I had been at the University of Memphis for almost three years, and that was my first time seeing him. Every female in the UC wanted his attention, but I was the only one that he was looking at. He was my first real boyfriend. When I was in high school there were dudes that I liked but none that were bold enough to try and talk to me because of my brothers.

Him: Nothing just wanted to tell you that I love you go ahead finish talking to your friend just call me when you get done or in the morning

Me: ok

After I finished texting him, I rolled over and drifted off to sleep. I was sleeping good as hell til Jabo's loud ass came in my room. I looked at the clock and seen that it was almost nine in the morning. I looked at him and wondered what the hell he could have wanted this early. Usually, I didn't get up until the afternoon, and he knew that. I made sure that I had all evening classes on Fridays. I didn't want to have to get up early and here his ass was waking me up.

"Jabo what is it?" I asked as I sat up in the bed.

"Damn yo brother can't come and talk to you. I haven't been here in a while, and I miss you," he told me getting in the bed and powering the TV on. I just fell back because all I wanted to do was sleep. I had a class at one, and I wanted to get some rest because I knew that I was going be on the go for the rest of the day. I got back comfortable so that I could go back to sleep. I knew that if he was cutting on the TV, he was going to fall to sleep as well.

"You finna go to sleep on me? " he asked. I knew right then that something was wrong.

"What's wrong Jabo?" I asked. He looked at me and dropped his head.

"So look I got a girl. She cool as shit. We just made shit official, this is new as fuck for me. I have never had to make the first move; usually, the females do that part?" he said looking stupid as hell. I didn't say shit I just laid there to see if he was going to keep talking. I don't know what he wanted me to say. "Main why you acting like you don't hear me," he questioned.

"I mean I don't know what you want me to say. You know damn well what you just said didn't make any sense. If she a real woman and not a hoe then she is not going to make the first move."

"Well, I don't know what to do. I don't want her to think that's all that I want. What we got is real, and I don't want to mess it up, but I need some pussy," he sadly said.

"Nigga let me find out yo ass in love and don't want to tell me." He looked at me like I had ten heads. I just laughed because he knew that what I was saying was true. He laid back like he had the stress of the world on his shoulders.

"Did you talk to Dub about this?" I laughed. I knew that he probably hadn't. Normally he came to me about all the shit that he didn't want to talk to Dub about. He knew that Dub was going to clown his ass.

"Bruh why you laughing and shit, it's not funny. The shit is fucked up. I don't get why females are so damn difficult. Then I called this morning and told her that I wanted to go out tonight, and she gone tell me that she was going to be busy. What the fuck was she going to be doing that would have her so busy," he asked me like I could tell him. Hell, I didn't even know the girl that he was talking about.

"Why don't you tell her how you feel? I'm sure that she would change if you tell her how you feel. She might even change her plans for you," I said just to see what he would say. That nigga jumped up and walked out of the room. I just shook my head and cut the TV off and rolled over. I knew that he was mad, but I didn't care. I fell back to sleep, and once again somebody woke me up bussing in my room. This time it was Dub.

"When were you gone tell me you was going out. And who

is this friend that you going with? I hope you not talking about Sam?" I rolled my eyes because I was tired of them treating me like I was a fucking kid.

"No, I'm not going with her. The friend that I'm going with works at the center. She's cool. Please let me go. I never get to be free. I just want to have some fun. Please Dub," I begged him. He gave me this look that I couldn't read. I knew then that he was going to say no. He walked out, and I got up to follow him. He was not going to do this to me. Even if he said no I was going to go.

"Russell Price," I yelled behind him. He stopped in his tracks and turned to me.

"Why you calling by my government like that Daeja," he angrily questioned. I just walked off because I knew he was going to wig out on my ass. I headed to my room so that I could calm down. When I picked up my phone, I noticed that it was almost noon and I had to be in class in an hour. I headed straight to my bathroom so that I could shower. When the hot water hit my body, I felt so relaxed. My mind went to my boo and realized that I hadn't talked to him. Normally I would have a text from him when I got up. I finished washing my body and got out. I went straight to my phone. Just like I thought he texted me. I texted him back and then texted Allia.

"You can go," Dub said walking in my room. I smiled because I just knew that I was going to have to sneak out. "Don't make me regret it Daeja. You need to make sure that yo phone stays charged and drive yo own car so that I will be able to track it," he told me. I ran over and hugged him. I was so damn happy. I wanted to twerk, but I didn't want him to change his mind. I ran in my closet in search of something to wear. I had so many choices since I never went anywhere but to the center and school. I wanted to wear something cute. I decide on a Gucci boyfriend tee and some fitted Gucci jeans. I slid on my Gucci slides and headed out the door. I prayed that class would be quick. I was so happy that I only had two weeks left before summer break. Traffic was heavy, so it took me forever to get to class. I was like ten minutes late. When I walked to the door, there was a note letting everyone know that class was canceled. I had like thirty minutes to spare so I headed to the library so that I could print some papers that I needed for class next week. Once I finished that and got in the car I called Allia to see if she wanted me to come and get her.

"Hey boo," she answered.

"I was calling to see if you wanted me to come and get you when I get out of class?"

"Naw boo I can meet you, Erin wants me to pick her up. I'm finna leave my house now she lives around the corner from me," she told me. We ended the call, and I pulled off from where I was parked. I decided to call my boo since I hadn't talked to him today. We had only texted.

"Hey baby," he answered sound sexy as always.

"Hey, love I was just calling to tell you that I was going to get something to eat with my friends. I had talked to you all day. How is your day going? " I asked.

"My day has been good. Just missing you."

"I miss you too baby," I assured him.

"Ok baby just make sure that you call me when you get there. I'm finna take care of some shit then I'm going to call you. You need some money?" He asked. He knew damn well that I didn't need no money. My brothers made sure that I had enough money. That didn't matter because he was still always giving me something. We ended the call, and I put the address for Houston's in the GPS and pulled off. I got there in no time. I rode around the parking lot looking for Allia's car. Just as I pulled into a space, she pulled up and parked beside me. We all got out at the same time.

"Hey boo," she greeted me. I hugged her. " This is Erin. Erin this is Daeja." We hugged and headed in the building. Erin was so damn pretty and let's not talk about her body. That mother-fucker was bangin'.

We were seated as soon as we walked in, which I was happy about. I was hungry as hell. My phone rang, so I searched my purse because I didn't know if it was my brother and I didn't want him to pop up. I knew that it was nobody but one of them. I had just talked to my boo, so I knew that he wasn't calling me. Whoever it was hung up and called right back. "Damn girl somebody really wants to talk to yo ass," Erin said causing us to laugh.

"Girl it was probably my damn brother. They be acting like my ass is ten years old." I finally found my phone and just as I thought it was my brother. I called him back, so I made sure that he didn't pop up because I knew that he was.

"I'm good. my phone was in my purse," I told him soon as I answered.

"You better be glad you found it because I was on the way to you." I knew that he was.

"Love you," I said before hanging up. I didn't want to hear him ask a million question. I looked up, and they were looking at me like I was crazy. "Please excuse me yall my brothers are kind of overprotective of me."

"It's ok girl hell I wish I had a brother," Allia said.

"Girl I swear you don't. They are so irritating. I can't do shit. They have my ass on lockdown, but I will say that they love me. I am thankful for them because I know that if I was living with my mom and dad, my ass would really be on lock."

"Girl be happy that you have people in your life that really love and care about you," Allia told me. I guess she was right, but I was tired of being treated like I was a kid. I was almost twenty, and I wanted to be treated like that

I loved my bothers, but I wish they would stop smothering me. I was a good kid; I didn't get in trouble. I made good grades and all. I knew that they did it because they loved me. I'm sure that they would have been mad if they knew that I had a boyfriend. I was so in love. I just wish that I could display the love that I had for him. He was my everything.

"So tell me about you Daeja?" Erin said as I texted my boo back.

"Well I'm nineteen I will be twenty in a few months. I have two brothers. I live with them as you know. I love kids. I'm in college majoring in children psychology. I have a boyfriend, but no one knows because my brothers are crazy. I don't have many friends except for this girl named Sam. She cool or whatever but I think that she's just around because she likes my brother."

"Aw ok cool. Well, I'm twenty-one, and I have a daughter her name is Eliza. I have an online hair boutique that I'm working on right now." We talked while we waited for our food. Erin was mad cool. I like her, and it seemed that she liked me. I was happy that I 've met such genuine people. We sat there talking for hours. It was damn near six by the time that we got ready to go. This was what I needed. There was so much that I couldn't talk to my brothers about.

11

———

ERIN

Lunch was great. I think that Daeja will fit in with us just fine. Since I was going out tonight, I had Allia to drop me off at my mother's house so that I could spend some time with my baby. When I walked into the house, and she was running, and my father was right behind her. I grabbed her and picked her up. She was laughing her little heart out. That warmed my heart. My baby was my everything. She was all that I could ask for. The only thing good that came out of fucking with Eli's dumb ass. I never knew that I could love someone this much. She was the reason that I had to let Eli go. I needed to be a good role model for my baby. I couldn't teach her to know her worth, and I didn't know my own. I wanted to be a great mother just like mines.

"Hey baby girl," my dad said kissing me.

"Hey, daddy. What you and this little monster doing.?" I asked putting Liza back down on the floor. She ran into the living room, and I followed her. My moms were on the couch making a blanket. That was her favorite thing to do. We had so many damn blankets. That was her thing so I would have as many as she gave me.

"Hey Mommy," I spoke taking a seat next to her. She looked up at me and smiled. She didn't have to say a word, but I knew that she was happy to see me.

"How was lunch baby?" She asked. My mother and I talked about everything, so she knew that I was going to meet Deaja for the first time. She knew that I didn't care for new people, especially when it come s to my bestie.

"It went well, mom. I really like her. It will be good to have someone new around to fill the void when Allia is at work. That's all her ass did anyway, and I knew that wasn't going to change especially since she said that she was done with Cell."

I just wanted to be a fly on the wall when she finally talked to that nigga. I knew that she probably had spoken to him, but she hadn't told me about it yet. It's been nearly a week since his ass got shot. She packed that nigga's shit up and took it to his mama. When she told me that shit, I thought she was playing, but she fooled me. She even got the locks changed. I was proud of her though, shit I needed to do the same thing. My baby daddy wasn't shit when he was on the street, and he ain't shit now, so I knew how she felt. I was so blessed that God chose me to be Eliza's mother, but I wish he would have chosen me different baby daddy.

"I made some lemon pie, go ahead and get you a piece so that you can give Eliza a bath and get her in the bed," my mother told me. I got up and did what she told me to do. I was so grateful for them. They loved Eliza so much. I knew that it was their job since they were her grandparents, but they didn't have to do as much as they do for her. It was like I had a second child for them. My mother nearly died having me, so she wasn't able to have more kids like she wanted to. Since the day that I had Eliza, she would say that she was her baby.

I cut me a piece of pie then sat at the table. I pulled my phone out and seen that I had five missed calls. I had five missed calls, one was from my bestie, and the others were from Jabo. I had no idea why he had called me that many times. Normally he would just call once. I thought about calling him back, but I decided to wait until I got home. Once I was done eating I headed to Eliza's room. She was sitting on the floor in her PJs. I guess my dad had already given her a bath while I was talking to my mother.

"What you watching Liza?" I asked taking a seat next to her. She had dolls spread out on the floor as always.

"YouTube," she simply stated. I had to laugh because he gave me a look as if I was bothering her. My baby was a mess. She was so grown and smart.

"Ok well once that video is over it bedtime little lady." She nodded and focused back on the TV. I decided to call Jabo back. I knew that he was going to talk shit, so I stepped outside just in case I had to curse his ass out.

"Yo, why the fuck you ain't been answering the phone," he damn near yelled in the phone.

"Ummm Why are you yelling and I was doing something," I told him. I knew that he was mad because he wasn't joking. What I didn't get was why he was mad. I told him what I was doing today. He knew where I was at. I texted him before I got here.

"Cause I needed you and you weren't answering." I pulled the phone from my face and looked at it. I was not with the checking in shit I was a grown ass woman.

"Joshua, I was busy. What did you need me for?" I knew that was going to piss him off more because he hated to be called by his government name.

"I'm on my way to your house you need to be there when I get there." was all he said before hanging up. I just shook my head because he was crazy as hell. I didn't worry about rushing because I knew that he would be at my house when I got there. I had no idea how he got a key, but he wouldn't give it to me, and I had stopped trying to get it.

An hour later I was headed home. I knew that he probably hadn't eaten, so I stopped and got us something from five guys. When I walked in the house, he was on the couch knocked out. He was so damn handsome, but I knew that we could never be together that nigga was the definition of a hoe. He had two bitches for every day of the week.

"Jabo get up," I yelled rocking him. His ass always slept hard as hell. I knew that he didn't sleep like that at home because when I would call, he would answer on the first ring whereas now he had damn near twenty missed calls.

"What mane?" he stirred in his sleep. I walked off so that I could put his food on a plate. When I came back, he was sitting up looking at this phone. I handed him the plate and sat next to him.

"Now what's wrong with you?" I asked taking a bite from my burger. He was still on his phone, so I took it from his hand and sat it on the table so that he could eat. He looked at me and then took a bite of his burger.

"I missed you," was all that he said. I didn't reply because that was what he always said. He finished his burger in no time, so that confirmed that he hadn't eaten. He got up and kissed me. I rolled my eyes because I hated when he did that shit. Now I was all hot and bothered. He walked to the back of the house, so I knew that he was going to shower. His ass acted as if he lived here. He made this his house like he didn't know that I had a nigga.

Me: what yall doing: A Boogie: shit sitting on the bed finna start on my makeup

Me: bitch you should have been doing that shit an hour ago you know you be taking all day

**P: Looking for something to wear. just got back from getting
my makeup done**
**Me: let me find out yo ass gone be fine don't have yo brother
trying to tag along**
**P: Girl please they ass not gone see me I'm going out the
back door**
A Boogie: lol yall crazy what time you picking us up P

P: 11

There was no need to reply I needed to get my shit together because I only had two hours and I was slow plus he was here, so I knew that he was going to have twenty-one questions. I walked into my room, and he was just coming out of the bathroom. He had on my pink robe, and as always I just laughed. It was actually kind of sexy. I walked in my closet so that I didn't have to keep looking at him. He was turning me on as always, but I couldn't find it in myself to cross that line.

I was looking for this black dress that I had purchased the other day when I felt his warm body against mines. A chill went through my body and caused me to moan.

"Damn I missed you," he mumbled in my ear.

"Sure you do," I said pulled away from him. This man was doing something to me, and I didn't like it.

"Why you acting like that. You know you miss a nigga," he said going to the small area that housed his clothes. I pulled my dress down and then grabbed the shoes that I planned to wear. "Where you going that you need to dress like that?" he asked. I didn't reply, I just walked off so that I could shower and get started on my makeup.

I didn't close the door because I knew that his ass would still come in here. I was done showering in no time. When I walked in my room, Jabo was standing by the window in nothing but his underwear. It's a good thing that my ass didn't have on panties because if I did, they would be ruined. He wasn't paying attention, so I walked my hot pussy ass right back in the bathroom. Only this time I closed the door.

"This nigga go have my ass around here throwing my ass in a circle," I mumbled as I pulled out my makeup. I knew that he was doing the shit on purpose because he did it all the time. I was so damn confused when it came to him. Once I was done with my makeup, I headed in my room so that I could get dressed. This time he was laid back in the bed. His cologne was invading my nose caused my center to drip. This man was so damn fine yall.

He walked over to where I was standing and kissed me. "Why do you do that?" I asked getting mad.

"Cause you my baby, and I wanted to kiss you. I'm finna head out I'm going out with my brother. I'm coming back here when I'm done," was all he said before walking off. I just shook my headed and finished getting dress because it was almost eleven.

I slipped my dress on and took a look at myself in the mirror. I was about to take a selfie, but I had a FaceTime come on. It was Jabo. I rolled my eye before answering.

"Yes," I answered with a fake smile. Damn, he was fine.

"Turn the camera around," I didn't as I was told. His facial expression was priceless. "Nah you need to change, wear some jeans or my sweats that are on the chair." I laughed and hung up on his ass. I hated it when he did that. I didn't need him telling me how to dress. I was a grown woman. That was shit that Eli used to do. When I had told him a million times that I was grown, and I was going to wear what I want. I grabbed my purse and clutch then headed to the living room so that I could switch my stuff over while I waited for them to pull up. I really wanted to drive, but Daeja's brother said that she had to drive her car. I was cool with that because that meant that I could get turned up.

12

ALLIA

I had been at home for damn near three hours, and now I was finally dressed and ready to party. I need this, so much had happened the past few weeks that I just needed a breather. I was getting dressed when my phone rang. It was an unknown number, so I decided to answer. I knew that it was probably someone just playing on my phone.

"Hello," I answered.

"So you blocked my number?" I took a deep breath because I really had been avoiding talking to him. There wasn't much for me to say. I had done all the talking that I needed to the last time that we talked. I knew that his ass was going to be calling I just didn't think that he would go as far as calling from someone else's number.

"Yes, I did. Cell, I've been asking for a baby for three years, and you kept telling me that it wasn't time. I stayed with you through a lot of shit but this, a baby, I can't do. I'm going to let you and her be happy. I'm done Cell," I didn't realize that I was crying up until tears started hitting my arm. I didn't have time for this bullshit. I never failed. It was like he knew when I was happy and he made it his business to call and ruin that.

"Look baby you know that I love you. I don't love her; she was a mistake."

"Mistake really Cell. That bitch was friendly with yo family. That bitch meant way more than me. You fucked up what we had. I gave you so many chances," I cried thinking about how many times I set niggas up just so that he could have money. Or when I rode around with drugs for him. Just thinking about it had me mad.

"Look you need to come off that shit you know what's up. You done put a nigga shit out like that ain't my shit too."

"Let's be clear this is my shit. I had it before I met you so miss me with that. Speaking of that when were you gone tell me that you hadn't paid the fucking rent. Two fucking months behind, if I hadn't been saving money my ass would be on the fucking street looking crazy. So you know what Cell, fuck you," I yelled before hanging up. He had me fucked up. I was in a bind because of him, and he thought that I had to be with him. I was good on him and any other nigga for that matter. I cleaned my face and redid my makeup, Deaja was calling to say that she was at the door. I made sure that you couldn't tell that I was crying and headed out. I knew that if she would have seen that I was crying that she would have started asking questions and I didn't need that right now. I wanted to enjoy this night and not think about his ass.

Once I made sure that I was good, I headed to the door. A big ass smiled crept on my face when I walked out the door and seen what we were riding in. I knew she had a Porsche, but I had never seen this truck. It was to die for.

"Hey boo," I greeted her as I got in the truck. She was all smiles, and that was one of the things that I loved about her. I hadn't ever seen her looking sad.

"What's up you ready to get turnt?" she joked. She knew damn well that getting turnt wasn't her thing. We pulled off headed to Erin's house. She was waiting at the door. My boo looked stunning. Soon as she got in the car, Deaja pulled out a blunt. I didn't even think that her ass smoked. I didn't complain or question it because after talking to Cell's ass I needed to smoke.

"I stole it from my brother he has so many laying around he will never notice that it's gone," she said lighting it at the stoplight. By the time it was gone we all were high as hell. I didn't smoke often, so I was lit.

We pulled up to Honey, a new strip club. It had only been open a few months. I had heard about it, but I hadn't had a chance to go. Hell, the whole city was talking about it. I had seen a few pictures on Instagram that was about it. Deaja pulled up to the front like she had been there before. I looked at Erin, and she just shrugged her shoulders. We got out and headed towards the door. The bouncer hugged her and then let us in the door. All of the people in the long ass line were looking at us crazy as hell.

"So I'm guessing you been here before," Erin asked as we walked through the door.

"Nope, my bothers own it." I looked back at Erin, and her face held the same expression as mines. Her brothers were going to think that we were a bad influence on her. She walked around like she had done this a million times. There were niggas pulling at us from all directions, but we all just kept walking. We stopped at the bar, and Dae ordered for us. "Can I have three vodka and cranberries," she told the bartender. The bartender just nodded and walked off to fix the drinks.

"Do yo brothers know you here?" the bartender asked her she just shrugged her shoulders. We each grabbed a drink and walked off. We made a way to where the dancers were and took a seat. It was a really nice club. It was very clean to say this was a strip club. Most strip clubs were run down no matter how new they were. The chairs didn't have stains and shit on them. I was impressed. The waiter came over as we were finishing up our first drink. Daeja put in an order for us another round as we danced to every song that came on. I was having so much damn fun. I felt like someone was looking at me. I looked around until I saw Cell's cousin. I knew that he was going to tell him that he saw me, but I didn't care. I was done with his ass. I grabbed my phone because I knew that he was going to be calling. Just as I thought he called ten damn times. Cell thought that I was just some dumb ass girl, but I was far from that. Now I will say that I was like that at first, but I knew better. I knew that he was no good for me. I just needed, to remember that. He had a way of changing my mind. I just knew that I was going to have to stay away from his ass.

"Give me this," Erin said taking my phone from me. I just rolled my eyes. I knew that she was going to do that. "We are here to have fun not think about Cell's bitch ass. Let that nigga see how you be feeling. He has ignored yo ass more time than we can remember. He needs to see that he had something good and fucked it up. Now down this drink, because we just placed another order," Erin said as she danced to the music. I downed the drink like she told me to and started back dancing. I knew that what she said was right, but I also knew Cell, and he was not going to let me go that easily.

13

DUB

I was sitting in my office getting topped off and watching the cameras. I could have sworn that I saw my baby sister. My eyes had to have been playing tricks on me. "Yo move," I said pushing one of the dancers named Shay's head out of my lap. She was one of the hoes that I let top me off here and there. I never fucked her because I didn't want her to think that it was something more than her giving me head.

"What's wrong baby?" she asked. I was so focused on the screen that I couldn't answer her. I tucked my dick back in and headed to see if I was seeing shit. Soon as I was walking out of my office, my brother was walking to his.

"Aye I think that I may be seeing shit, but I think that I just saw Deaja and Erin in the club," I told him. I turned around and went back to my office with him following behind me. This time I was able to get a better look. Not only was Deaja in the club she was with the girl that hit my damn car and Erin. It was niggas all over the section that they were sitting in. Hell, they were getting more attention than the damn dancers.

"Naw hell naw," was all Jabo said before walking out of my

office. I followed behind him. That nigga was walking fast as hell.

"Yo, yall niggas got a half a fucking second to get the fuck from over here before ya mammies be pulling out their black dresses." Them niggas scattered so damn fast I had to keep from laughing. One of the niggas damn near fell.

"Daeja what are you doing here?" was the first thing that came out of my mouth. "And what are you doing with her?" I asked. Ole girl looked at me like I had grown a second head right in front for her. I didn't get why she was mad because she was the one that had hit my car. Hell, I should have been the mad one.

"How yall gone tell me that I can go out with my friends as long as it wasn't Sam and then act like this. Come on yall we can just go somewhere else," Daeja said looking like she was getting ready to cry. That shit made a nigga feel bad as fuck. I looked over at Jabo, and he was giving Erin the look of death, but she wasn't paying that any attention she was on her phone. I looked at Erin and knew why he was mad.

"Mane look come on. Yall can't be down here with these broke motherfuckers." I let them walk off first. I wanted to hear what Jabo was saying to Erin, but they were walking slow and shit. I looked back at them and realize why his ass was so damn mad. Hell if she wasn't my brother's girl, I would definitely be trying to get at her.

"Yo I thought I told you not to wear that shit," he asked her.

"I told you that I'm grown. I can wear what I want if I would have known that she was your sister trust me, I wouldn't have come. I'm sure there are plenty of ho's that would love for you to try and run there life, but I'm not beat for that shit," She walked off and caught up with my sister and Allia.

Allia was just as fine as I thought she was. And all that ass she had on the back of her had my dick jumping. I knew that she had to have a nigga because there was no way a woman that fine was single. Her ass didn't even look my way which was different for me. Every female that I came in contact with wanted me, but she was acting like a nigga didn't exist. When we made it up to the VIP area, they didn't waste any time fixing drinks. I knew that Daeja drank, so that didn't bother me. I just took a seat in the corner and watched Allia. I knew that she felt me watching her because she looked like she was uncomfortable. I wanted to say something to her, but I wasn't about to take a chance on her shooting a nigga down.

I walked over and before I could get close to her Daeja stopped me. "Nope Dub these are the first friends that I have found that are my friend for me and not for yall so yall not finna run them away. Jabo already all over Erin." I just looked at her because she was dead ass serious.

"Aye, I just want to ask her about my car. That's the female that I was telling you hit my car," I said watching her like she was my prey. Daeja just walked off because she knew that she wasn't going to win this one. I grabbed my bottle of water and walked over to her.

"I hope you done figured out how you gone pay for my car?" I asked walking up in her personal space.

"Ummm nigga you done lost yo mind. I'm not getting shit fixed, hell I haven't even got my shit fixed. So if that's what you came over here for you can take yo ass right back over there. Besides I'm sure that if you own this place that you can afford to get your car fixed," she said not even looking my way. That shit turned me on. I grabbed her a pulled her closer to me. She gave me the ugliest look.

"Nigga get off me," she said pushing me off her. I just laughed and scooted over. I sat back and looked at my sister she was dancing having the time of her life, that shit made a nigga feel bad. A nigga felt like he was protecting her by keeping her out the streets and away from fuck niggas but it looks like I did more harm than anything. She was my heart, and I couldn't stomach anything happening to her. Hell, she didn't even have a boyfriend as far as I knew. She was a good kid, and I wanted to keep it that way. I didn't want her around here being a hoe like her friend Sam. I was so busy looking at my sister that I didn't not that Allia got up and started dancing with Daeja.

"Bruh this shit crazy," Jabo whined like he was a big ass baby. I just laughed because lil mama had that nigga pressed.

"Yo, what the fuck is funny?" he asked. I just looked at him because the only time that I saw him like this was when money was missing. She had that nigga acting a fool. She was up with Daeja and Allia dancing. That nigga's eyes didn't leave her ass.

"Nigga, you here with her chill?" I told his ass. I could see if he wasn't here, but he was so she was good.

"That ain't the point. What if I wasn't what if she would have been somewhere else." I wanted to press the issue just to fuck with him, but out the side of my eye, I saw Allia coming to sit next to me. She had a few drinks, so she was damn near falling over. Hell, I was happy that she was coming to sit next to me. At first, she didn't want a nigga near her. Just as she was sitting down, she dropped her phone. I used that as my chance to put my number in her phone. She was so busy trying to sit down that she didn't notice that she dropped it. I saw that she had a lot of missed calls. That didn't concern me though. She sat there for a minute then got back up and started dancing when Cardi B came on.

They looked like they were having so much fun. It wasn't often that I saw my baby sister smile this much. Just as I was getting up so that I could go and check on the rest of the club, Sam walked up. I looked at Deaja. She knew that I didn't fuck with that hoe and by the look on Erin and Allia's face they didn't either.

"Nah lil mama you can't chill up here," I told her. She looked at me like I had said some wrong shit. She just walked off. I knew that she wanted to say something crazy, but she knew better. Once I made sure that she was gone I headed to my office so that I could get a good view of the whole club. I wanted to be all in Allia's face, but I had a business to run. It was packed as always. Me and my brother had done a good job with this place. We were the hottest in the city. There were people everywhere. I sat at my desk and watched Allia. I was going to make her mines no matter if she wanted to be or not. I had a lot of paperwork that I needed to get done, so I took the time to do that. Just as I was finishing up, there was a knock at my office door.

"Come in."

I looked up to see my baby mama. She was looking good as fuck. She walked in and locked the door behind her. I knew what that meant, she came to get some dick. As bad as I wanted to fuck her I knew that I didn't need to. She did understand that a fuck was just a fuck. She gone think a nigga was ready to be back with her and shit.

"I miss you and him," she gushed as she pulled on my pants. I stopped her because my dick was getting hard. If my shit got too hard, there was no going back.

"Roz you know we can't go there," I told her. She stopped and just looked at me. I could tell that her feelings were hurt.

"Never mind I don't know why I wasted my time," she said walking out of my office. I really felt bad, but I didn't need that drama in my life. Plus my mind was on Allia. I needed her in my life, and I was going to get just that one way or another.

14

JABO

I sat back and watched Erin, my sister and Allia have the time of their lives. They were partying like they didn't have a care in the world. I had been telling Dub that we had been too hard on Daeja. He didn't see it that way.

I could help but to watch Erin. My bae was so fucking beautiful. I don't know who Erin thought that she was, but she had me fucked up with that dress on. All that dress was going to get her was some dick. I told her that I didn't want her wearing that shit, but she still wore it like what I said didn't mean shit. She knew how a nigga felt about her, but she was always trying to play me to the left. It was like she couldn't see shit my way. She wasn't single, and that dress that she was wearing said otherwise. I didn't want to have to body anyone tonight but the way she was dressed that was bound to happen.

"Aye let me holla at you," I said to Erin as she was walked over to sit with my sister and her friend.

"What is it Jabo?" she asked as if I was getting on her nerves. That kind of hurt a nigga's feelings because she knew how a nigga felt about her. She was mine, and she was going to act as such.

"I just want you next to me." She gave me this look that I couldn't read and sat down. I knew that she loved a nigga she didn't have to tell me. I knew that I loved her ass the same damn way. I just need to find it in myself to be the man that she needed me to be.

My phone vibrated in my pocket pulling me from thoughts. I saw that it was Dub calling, so I answered.

"Aye tell ole girl come holla at me." I just shook my head because Daeja was going to be in her feeling about her friends. I knew that for a fact she was such a baby. I understood though. Most females just wanted to be her friend because she was our sister thinking that was going to get them some brownie points.

"My brother said he needs you to look at something for him." She gave me the 'nigga please' look then turned back to my sister like I hadn't said anything. I knew that he was looking because Flip, one of the bouncers, was walking over. He didn't even say shit to her; he just picked her up and carried her off. She was yelling, but no one could hear her because of the loud music.

My sister and Erin were just looking because they knew that it was nothing they could do. I looked over at my sister, and she was smiling in her phone. That shit didn't sit right with me. I knew that it had to have been a nigga cause it was late as hell. I made a mental note to look into it. If my sister was messing with someone, then I needed to know. I knew that she didn't want to tell me because she thought that I was going to be mad, but I wasn't as long as it wasn't a fuck nigga.

"I'm ready to go," Erin said as she leaned on me. She was drunk as hell.

"You ready to go too?" I asked Daeja. She was so into her phone that she didn't hear me, so I snatched the phone out her hand.

"Jabo what are you doing?" she yelled. She was trying her

hardest to take the phone from me. It was actually funny as hell.

"You so into this phone that you act like you can't hear. Now you can tell me who you texting or I can go and tell Dub. Your choice."

"Ok I will tell you in the car just give me my phone," she whined. I handed her the phone, and we all headed out. I didn't worry about Allia because she was good with Dub. When we made it to the car, I realized that Daeja had driven her car.

Me: We out, drive Dae's truck home: Dub D: Ok

I made sure that the both of them were in the car then headed to drop Daeja off. I was going to stay at Erin's house tonight. I looked over, and Erin's ass was already knocked out. I knew then that she was fucked up because she hated sleeping in the car and she was out cold.

"I'm listening Dae." I looked through the mirror, and she was rolling her eyes. I just laughed because she knew that I wasn't going to let it go.

"It's a guy that I go to school with damn."

"Name?"

"I will tell you if you tell me the girl's name that you're in love with." I had to stop so that I could look at her to be sure that she had just said that like Erin wasn't in the car. Hell, I'm happy that she was sleep. "Well, I'm listening."

I looked over at Erin, and she was knocked out. I then looked back at Daeja and nodded towards Erin. The look on Daeja's face was priceless.

"I'm never going to have any friends," was all she said before looking back at her phone. I knew that she was going to be mad, but a nigga couldn't help the way I felt. Erin was my happiness. Honestly, she was all that I wanted. If I could have her, I would throw in my playa card no questions asked. The only thing was I wasn't ready to do that. Erin was very headstrong, so she wasn't going for that shit. She didn't take my shit. That was what made me want her. Outside of that, she was smart beautiful and a great mother.

The rest of the ride Dae was on her phone, and I was thinking about how I was going to get my shit in line. Just as I was getting off the e-way my phone buzzed, it was Gram.

"Yo," I answered.

" I just did the last pick up. I'm headed in. I will do the count in the morning," he advised me.

"Ok cool. We just left the club. I'm going to be in for the night. Just call me if you need me," I told him before ending the call. I looked back at my sister, and she was falling asleep. I knew that was going to happen because she was drunk as hell.

When we pulled in the house, I helped my sister out of the car and made sure that she got in the house. I locked the door behind myself then got back in the car and headed to Erin's house. A nigga was sleepy as hell. I just wanted to lay down.

I pulled in the driveway then shut the car off. I knew that I was going to have a hard time getting her ass out of the car. I put my phone in my pocket and got my keys to her house out. I opened the door and prayed that she wasn't laying on it. Once I opened it, she woke up and smiled. I unbuckled her seat belt and helped her stand up. Once we were in the house, she started to undress right at the door. My dick was getting harder by the second.

"Come and help me," she demanded. I had no idea what she needed my help with because her ass was already naked. I walked in the room, and she was laying on the bed with her legs wide open. I was stuck. I was not expecting that at all.

"What you need my help with Erin?" I asked because she was playing and I didn't have the time.

"With this." She rubbed her finger across her clit, and that was the sexiest shit ever. I made my way over then moved her hand.

"You sure this is what you want to do?" I asked.

"I thought you was my man. My man wouldn't ask any questions," she told me as she pulled me in for a kiss. Her kisses were intoxicating. I could kiss on her all day. We pulled away from our kiss, and she laid back so that I could take control. I pulled her close to the end of the bed. I wanted to get a good look at what was now mine. I slowly kissed from her toes to the middle of her legs. I wanted to make sure that I touched every inch of her body. When I made it to her pussy, I softly kissed it. I looked up so that I could see if she was looking down at me. When I saw that she was, I attached my mouth to that pussy like it was my first and last meal.

"Shit baby what are you doing to me," she moaned out. I just smiled because I knew that I was fucking her head up worse than it already was. If she wasn't in love, she would be today. I ate her pussy till her legs were so weak that she couldn't hold them up.

"I wanna feel that dick inside of me," she demanded. I crawled up on the bed and gave her just that. I eased my dick inside of her, and instantly I was in heaven. I knew then that she was the one for me. Her shit fit around my dick like a glove. It felt so good that I had to make love because I wanted to be inside her for as long as I could.

"Damn baby, shit," I moaned out. She was moving her hips which made me stop moving. She was fucking me like no other, I felt my nut rising, so I stopped her and made her flip over. I entered her slowly. I could feel her body get tense and then relax once I was completely inside of her. I thought that would help me go longer, but soon as I started moving, I released all inside of her.

We both fell down on the bed. She looked and me and started smiling. "What you smiling like that for?" I asked.

"Oh, I just wanted you to see the smile that will be on my face when I kill yo if you cheat on me," she said before kissing me and getting up. What the fuck did I get myself into?

15

____

ALLIA

I couldn't believe that this nigga really had his security to come and get me. When I made it to his office, he was sitting there looking like a snack. Naw, fuck that he was looking like a damn three-course meal. He was so damn fine. I knew that my drinks would take over and that was part of the reason that I didn't want to come up here. I didn't know what the hell he was going to do to me. I had fucked up his expensive ass car. I was kind of happy that he let me leave because my insurance would have really gone up if I would have filed a claim.

"So what we gone do about my car?" he asked as soon as I sat down. I had really had a lot to drink, my ass damn near missed the chair. I was fucked up, and he was asking me about a damn car.

"Um, I'm sure that you have more than enough money. We talked about this," I said as I adjusted myself. He was watching me like I was his prey and that was making me uncomfortable as hell.

"Why you so mean?" he smiled. Oh Lord, that smile. Everything about this man was turning me on just by looking at him.

I made a mental note to curse Erin and Dae out for just letting this nigga take me. They ass hadn't even checked on me.

"I'm not mean I just don't have time for bullshit." He looked at me and smiled. I knew then that he was going to be a pain in my ass.

"Let's get out of here," he said just as his phone rung. I really couldn't hear what he was saying, all I know is that he turned around and grabbed some keys that were on his desk and we walked out. When we got outside, we walked to Daeja's truck. The soft leather seats felt so good against my body.

"You hungry?" he asked me. I didn't look his way. I just nodded my head. I don't know why I felt so comfortable being around him, but I did. I had no idea where we were headed. I felt my phone vibrate, it was Cell. I had been ignoring his ass because there was nothing that we had to talk about. I was done with his ass. Soon as I hit ignore he called right back. Dub took the phone from my hand. I didn't even have the energy to say nothing. I just let him do his thang.

"What's good?" he answered.

"Yo, who the fuck is this and where is Allia?" Cell asked.

"She busy right now. She gone holla at you later," he said. My eyes were closed, but I heard him drop the phone in the cup holder. I knew that Cell's ass was probably having a fit. I wouldn't be shocked if the nigga didn't have someone at my house to see if I was there. I made a mental note to start looking for somewhere else to stay because he was not going to leave me alone.

"You want Waffle House, or you want my chef to make you something?" he asked. I opened my eyes to make sure that he was serious. It was four in the morning I just wanted to eat.

"Chef," was all I said before closing my eyes back. It felt like we were riding forever. I didn't realize that I had fallen asleep until I felt him scooping me up out the car. I opened my eyes to see the most beautiful house that I had ever laid my eyes on.

He was struggling to hold me and open the door, so I took the key from him and unlocked the door. He sat me on the couch, and I swear to you that I felt like I was in heaven. I wide awake now, so I watch as he moved around his house. I heard a female's voice and got in defense mode until I realized that it was Daeja. She came down the stairs in a robe. She was on her phone as always. That damn girl would die without that phone.

"Bitch let me find out," she said sitting next to me.

"What I tell you about yo mouth Dae," Dub said. I just laughed because you could tell that she was his baby. She just rolled her eyes. He walked over and handed us both a plate. I dug straight in. I was hungry as hell. Dub walked up with a bottle of water and some pills. I took them from him and downed the bottle of water. Soon as he walked off, Daeja followed behind. She had this look on her face that I couldn't read.

I had sobered up, so the nosey me want to hear what she was about to say to him. I waited until they were in the hall before I got up.

"Dub what are you doing? Jabo said that you were taking her home. She is my only real friend," Porsha said sounding like she was going to cry.

"Dae what are you talking about?" he asked lost.

"She is the only person that I have met that's my friend for me. She doesn't have a motive like everyone else. You are overstepping with her. If you fuck up then not only will she be out of your life she will be out of mines. The same goes for Jabo. Yall just have no fucking boundaries."

"Ok, Dae. I will back up just don't cry," he damn near begged. That was so sweet to me. I had heard all that I needed to hear so I made my way back to where I was so that they wouldn't know that I was listening. I understood what she was saying because that was one of the things that we talked about. She would always tell me how she had no friends. I really didn't know much about her brother. Hell, I didn't realize that Erin knew her other brother. This was all new to me. One thing that I did know was that she loved her brothers. So there was no way that I would mess with Dub. He was fine as hell, but there was no way that I could do Daeja like that. Since they were still talking, I grabbed the remote so that I could find me something to watch on tv. Just as I was getting comfortable Daeja came in the living room and grabbed my hand. When we walked up the stairs to what I guess was her room, it was almost the size of my whole apartment.

"Damn bitch do you need any more room?" I asked as I took a seat on the couch. This girl had a full living room inside her bedroom. I knew that she had money, but I swear I didn't expect this.

"Girl please this room is small compared to the one at our old house."

"Well, this is the size of my whole apartment," I told her. She just laughed. One thing that I loved about her was the fact that she was humble. If you didn't know her you wouldn't know was that she was rich. She had the sweetest heart, and I loved that. Soon as my head hit the pillow, I was knocked out.

16

CELL

"Yo why the fuck you staring at me," I asked my baby mama. I guess she thought that shit was going change because Allia was mad at me. I had been calling Allia since last night, and her ass wasn't answering. This bitch wasn't making me feel any better because she was looking at me like I was crazy. She knew what was up with Allia and me before she got pregnant by a nigga. Allia was playing with me, and she knew what was up with me. My nigga told me that he saw her at the club last night and then some nigga answered her phone.

"I'm just trying to see why you so worried about her. I'm the one that has been here for you. Her ass hadn't been to see you period," Nia fussed. I knew that she was going to say that because she had been saying that all damn week. She was saying it like I didn't know that Allia hadn't been here. Tia and I have been rocking for a while, but I never intended on getting her pregnant. She knew that I didn't want a kid, so she waited until it was too late to tell me that she was pregnant. I had a fucked-up childhood, so there was no way that I wanted to bring a child in this shit. My mama left my ass when I was ten, and I have been getting it on my own since. Allia is the only person that I loved. Although Tia has been around longer she never really gave a nigga a reason to love her. She was cool, but she was just like every other female, a gold digger. She always had her hand out. But Allia was nothing like that. My baby was a go-getter. No matter how much money I had coming in, she still got up and took her ass to work. She made sure that the house was clean and a nigga had a good meal every night.

"That's your fucking fault when you saw her you should have sat yo ass down and played yo role," I yelled. I was mad as hell when my sister told me that she approached Allia. Anyone that knew me knew that I didn't play about her.

"You know what, fuck you. That bitch needed to know what the fuck was up. You keep me in the background like I just came around. I was here way before her ass. You want to be mad at me for standing up for myself. I'm the one that's having your child not her. I'm gone make sure you don't come calling me when that bitch kicks yo ass to the curb. If you think that she gone take yo ass back after finding out about me you a fool," she yelled as she grabbed all of her shit and walked out the room. I just laid and let what she said sink in. Allia loved me, so I knew that she was just acting out because she was mad. There was no way that she would leave me. I was all she knew. I made sure of that went I killed her old ass grandma. She stayed in my business too much. Every time a nigga cheated she was telling Allia to leave me. Hell, I wanted to off her hoe ass friend, but she was my nigga's baby mama. That was the only reason that she was still alive.

I picked up my phone and called her again. This time she answered. " So you got niggas answering yo phone now?" I asked soon as she answered.

"What do you want Cell? I'm tired, and I have a hangover. Don't you got a baby mama to worry about?" she asked. I just held the phone because she wasn't acting like herself. My Allia would never talk to me like that. I knew that she was hurt, but this was the first time that a nigga had cheated. She knew that I had other hoes so why was she acting like it was new to her.

"Yo what the fuck is up with you. You talk to me like I ain't shit."

"Because you not. Now, what is it that you want I was trying to sleep, and you are keeping me from doing that. I will call you if I feel like talking later other than that leave me alone and go be with yo baby mama," she said then hung up. I could believe this shit. I can't believe she was really trying to play me like I was a fuck boy. She knew me better than that. I was going to show her ass though. Soon as I get out of here, I was going to show her the type of nigga I really was.

I called my nigga Slim to see if he found the nigga that damn near killed my ass. I had been hearing that it was some nigga that I grew up with. I really was the one to blame. I talked around the wrong nigga. The city was run by the Price brothers. My nigga from Atlanta came down, and he was going to take over. He fucked with me tough. He had even bought a shop for me to run. No one really knew that the shop wasn't mines.

"What nigga?" Slim answered. That was one thing that I didn't like that nigga talked like he was above everyone. If it wasn't for the money I made by fucking with him, I would have killed his smart mouth ass by now.

"I was just calling to see if you heard anything yet?" He told me that he was looking for who shot me, but it had been well over a week, and I hadn't heard from his ass. I needed to know that when I left here, I would be safe. One of the young niggas from the hood said that he thinks that Dub, one of the Price brothers set that shit up. That nigga's reach was far, but he was like the rest of us. He had me fucked up if the thought that I was just going to let this shit ride.

"Have I called you nigga? Don't be calling questioning me," he said before hanging up in my face. I just looked at the phone because what he didn't know was as soon as I helped him kill Dub and Jabo I was going to kill his ass.

I rolled over so that I could go to sleep just as my phone rang. It was Slim, and I debated if I wanted to answer since the nigga had just hung up in my face. He hung up and called back after that, so I knew that he wanted something.

"Yea."

"Corry got the sister to meet him. If we can get her, then we can get the nigga to hand it all over to me. I need you to get better and get out so we can work on the second part of the plan," he said as if I knew what the second part was.

"Aite was all that I said. I didn't know what he wanted me to say because I had no idea what part two was and I didn't care. I just wanted the money that was going to come. I didn't care about shit else.

17

———

DEAJA

A FEW DAYS LATER

I stood in the mirror in my room making sure that I was looking good. I was headed to meet with my new boo. I knew that my brothers were out doing they thing so I wouldn't hear from them unless I called them. I met Corry one day a while back when I was in the bookstore at school. He was so damn sexy. He was 6'3 with tattoos all over his body. When he approached me, I knew that I should have turned him down, but he was just so damn fine. Then to top that he was a real live gentleman. He opened doors and all that.

I made sure that my makeup was still good because I had gotten it done earlier in the day. Once I made sure that I was all good I headed out the door. I was dressed in a pair of high waist jeans a pink crop top, and a pair of YSL pumps. Ya girl was looking good. I decided to pull my Range out today. My brother got me one like his because he got tired of me driving his. I plugged the address that he sent me in the GPS and then pulled off. I was listening to Meek Mills. As I made my way there, my mind drifted off to Gram's fine ass. He reminded me so much of Meek. He hated when I said that but it was the truth. Gram was the perfect man for me, but I knew that my brothers would never see it that way. I pulled up at the address that he gave me then called him.

"I'm outside," I told him soon as he answered.

"Aite baby I finna come outside," he said before hanging up. I sat there waiting for him to come out of the house. He walked out after like twenty minutes. I grabbed my purse and phone before getting out and locking my car behind me. He grabbed my hand, and a nervous feeling came over me. That slowed my pace. I had no idea what it was about this house, but something wasn't right. I wanted to turn my ass around and get back in my car, but I also wanted to spend time with him. I don't get why we couldn't spend time at a hotel or something. Why did we have to be at someone else's house

"You good baby?" he asked me as we walked on the porch. I gave him a forced smile and nodded. When we walked into the house, I looked around. It was nicely decorated, but it didn't look homey. It almost looked as if someone had just moved in it. I took a seat on the couch not wanting to get comfortable. In my mind, I kept hearing my brother tell me that if I wasn't comfortable that I needed to call one of them or leave. I knew that I couldn't call them, so I needed to think of a reason to leave.

"Whose house is this?" I asked.

"My folks," he told me. I just nodded as he pulled me closer to him. I wanted a direct answer I needed a name, but I knew that I couldn't ask that. I sat there looking around. He kept looking at the door that led to what I guess was the hallway. That was weird to me. He got up and walked out of the room. I used that as my opportunity to text Allia. There was something about how he was acting that was throwing me off. I knew that she would tell me what to do.

**Me: I'm with new boo I feel weird something not right about how
he acting
Big Sis A: Well you need to leave**

Me: Ok

I knew that she was going to call me in a minute. I just needed to wait it out. I was going to use that as an excuse to leave.

"What up though baby? I thought you missed a nigga," he smiled as he walked back in the room. Normally we would meet at a public place, but he really wanted me to come here. I had hadn't ever felt this uncomfortable around him. Maybe it was because I wasn't in public. This was way to enclosed for me. I wish that I wouldn't have come, but I was here now.

"I do miss you," I told him honestly. He knew how I felt about him. He rubbed up against my leg, and that was a no go. He knew that I wasn't going to have sex unless I was married. I had explained that several times. I stopped him just as his hand made it to my private area. I scooted over, and he gave me a look that I couldn't read.

"Damn I can't touch on what's mine?" he asked. I gave a faint smile then moved his hand once again. He was getting ready to talk but my phone rung. It was Allia calling. I answered fast so that he could chill out because I was feeling unconformable.

"Hello," I answered as if I didn't know that she was going to call.

"It's an emergency I need you to come home," she lied. I made sure that the phone was up loud enough for him to hear. That's what I love about her; she knew what to do and when to do it.

"What's wrong?" I asked as if it really mattered. I even jumped up as if something had really happened. I just wanted to leave here.

"I have to go," was all I said before getting up and heading to the door. I made sure that I was moving too fast for him to stop me. While I was walking to the car, I was still talking like something was wrong. I didn't even give his ass time to say bye before I pulled off. I could see his ass through the mirror looking at me. I knew that he was going to be calling but what he didn't know was his ass was going to be blocked. I was done because something wasn't right about his ass. I don't know how I didn't see the shit. I guess I wanted to have a boyfriend so bad that I was looking over all of that.

"Girl I'm gone thanks because that nigga was on some other shit. We have been around each other plenty of times I don't know how I didn't see this shit earlier," I told her. I was mad at myself because I didn't pay enough attention. I knew better.

"I told you that nigga was weird as hell. When you told me that he be asking about yo brother, I knew something was up with him. Niggas don't ask about other niggas. That shit is suspect as hell if you ask me," she pointed out. I told her the other day that he was always asking about my brother constantly. Like we couldn't have one conversation and he not bring them up. I said something about it, and he stopped. That was the only reason that I was still fucking with him. I liked him. I just didn't know if it was because he was bold enough to try and get at me knowing who my brothers were or if I just really liked him. Allia and I talked the rest of the way to my house. I kept looking back because I felt like someone was following me. I didn't see anything out the norm, so I just kept driving. I was happy when I pulled up and didn't see my brothers. I knew that I was going to have to tell them what happened because something was telling me that I would be seeing him again. Corry swore that he was in love with me, so there was no way that he was just going to let me stop talking to him.

I ended the call with her as soon as I pulled in the driveway and headed in the house. I went straight to my room. I cut on my beats pill then headed to shower. Before doing that I blocked Corry's number. I was done with him. I think that if Allia hadn't called me, he would have tried something, and I wasn't with that shit.

I sang along with Monica's *For You I will*, as I showered. I was the biggest Monica fan. Once I felt that I was clean, I grabbed my robe and shut the shower off. I looked for my favorite body mist, but I didn't see it. I knew that it could only be one other place and that was on my dresser. I grabbed my phone walked into my room to look for it.

"I thought you had an emergency," I heard the last voice that I wanted to hear. I damn near jumped out my damn skin. I had my back to him. I wanted to turn around, but I was trying to think about what I did with my gun. I thought that I had one on my dresser, but I'm sure that he looked around for one before I came out of the bathroom.

"What are you doing in my room? How did you even get in my house?" I questioned as I made my way to the light switch. When I cut the lights on that nigga was laid back in my bed like he paid the damn bills.

"I don't know how you got in my house, but you need to find your way out, before my brothers come home," I told him.

"I thought you said that they don't be here during the day?" he smirked. I knew that I shouldn't have told him that. That's what my ass gets for talking and thinking that I was grown. I had singlehandedly led this nigga here. I inched my way to where I kept my spare gun. The one that was on my dresser was already gone so I need to get closer to another one. Normally it would be in my nightstand, but I had it in my purse because I was at his house, or whoever house it was.

"I already took your gun out your purse, and I got the one that was on the dresser if that's what you are looking for," he said shocking me. I had one more gun, but it was in the closet. I stood there thinking about how I was going to get to it.

"What do you want Corry?" I asked. I was scared as shit, but there was no way that I was going to let his ass know that. I made my way around the room as if his ass wasn't in here. I wanted to get some clothes on more than anything. I grabbed some panties out the drawer. I didn't look to see what kind I just slipped them on the I slid on some pants. He was watching me like a hawk.

"Damn you don't want me to see your body?"

"Cory I don't even want your creepy ass in my house. Can you please leave," I said getting mad. I should have listened to Allia. I knew as soon as I walked in my closet that he was walking closer. I could feel his energy get up from the bed. That meant that he was making his way behind me. I walked to the back of the closet so that I could grab the box that held my other gun. Soon as I grabbed the box, he took it from my hand. I tried to turn around, but he grabbed me by my hair and dragged me out of the closet. That shit hurt so bad. I wanted to cry, but I couldn't do that because then he would know that I was scared. My brother always told me what to do in the situations, but it was like my mind was blank. Honestly, I never knew that some shit like this would happen.

"Let me see that little pussy," he said grabbing the shorts that I had just slipped on. At that point I couldn't fake it anymore I was terrified. I tried pushing him off me, but he was too strong. He jammed his finger up my private and I could help but to cry out. I laid there and prayed that one of my brothers would come home. Soon as he pulled his pants down, some nigga called his name. He snatched me from the floor and dragged me out of the room with him. Soon as we walked out of the room, I threw my hand over my mouth. My house was a mess. It was people going all through our house. I couldn't help but cry.

"What nigga?" he asked the guy.

"Mane we ain't found shit but a few thousand dollars," He

told him and that's when I noticed that Corry's eyes went to the hallway that Dub's office was on. I guess the dude read his mind because he told him that they couldn't get in the room. I wanted to laugh because the guy's face looked defeated. Cory dropped me to the floor and walked towards the door. "Watch her," he told the guy. I was right across from the table that my brother always kept a gun under it. They had guns all over the house. The guy was on his phone, so he didn't see me. Just as I was feeling for it, Cory came back down the hallway.

I sat straight up so that he wouldn't notice what I was doing. I looked at him and wondered where the guy that I had gotten to know was. This was a whole other person. I guess it was like my brother always told me. People are never who they seem to be.

I sat back and watched him pace the floor as if he was trying to figure something out. I knew that he could feel me looking at him, but it was as if he didn't want to look my way. "What I do so bad to you? How could you tell someone that you love them and then try to hurt them? Just answer that for me Corry" I asked. He stopped pacing and looked at me as if I was the scum of the earth. He turned his back which gave me time to scoot a little more. Just as I was feeling for the gun again, he grabbed me and dragged me to my brother's office.

"Open the door," he demanded. I just looked at him because he was a fool if he thought that I was going to do that. I guess me looking at him like that made him mad because the next thing that I knew I was blacking out.

18

DUB

A FEW DAYS LATER

"Shit baby suck my dick just like that," I moaned out as Bri swallowed my seeds. I swear this girl was the queen of sucking dick. I couldn't name a time that she left me unsatisfied. Once she made sure that she sucked me clean, I laid back on the bed and watch her ass jiggle as she headed to the bathroom. She closed the bathroom door, so I pulled out my phone so that I could call Gram. I had that nigga looking into some shit for me. A week or so ago, a nigga thought that it was a good idea to try and rob me. I popped both of the niggas I just didn't know if they were alive or not. I had Gram to have the female that he was messing with that worked at the hospital to see if anyone came in shot up, but she said that she hadn't heard anything. I had no idea who the niggas were, but I was going to find out. Word on the streets was that it was some niggas that were from Atlanta lurking around. I had been running shit in Memphis for too long for a nigga to think that he was going to come and take some shit from me.

"What's good nigga?" he answered.

"Shit I was calling to see if you heard anything yet," I asked. I knew that he was going to get mad, but I didn't care. I know that I hadn't given him time to do his thing, but it had been over a week. He should have something by now.

"Nigga I told you don't keep calling me about that shit. I'm going to take care of it don't worry. Go and get some pussy or something because you doing too much," he said as if that was going to make me feel better.

"Fuck you," was all that I could say. I just hung up because I knew that my conversation was going to go left. I got up so that I could shower and headed to the warehouse. I needed to change some shit around. Every few months I did that just so shit like what happened last week wouldn't happen. I didn't need anyone knowing my moves. I also needed to go up to the club to make sure shit was good there. We had a party this weekend, so I wanted to make sure that we had enough liquor.

"So am I going to see you later?" she asked. I just nodded. I knew that I wasn't going to see her, but she didn't need to know that. I made sure that I never spent too much time with her because I didn't need her thinking that this was more than a fuck.

"Well, I get off at midnight. I will leave the door unlocked for you," she said. I just stepped inside the bathroom to finish washing up, so that I could head out. Once I made sure that I was good I left. When I made it to my car, I called my sister. I hadn't talked to her all day, and that was unusual. She didn't answer, so I called Jabo to see if he was home to make sure that she was good. Just as I was dialing his number, I was pulling up at the warehouse, and his car was outside. I just shut my car off and headed in to see if he had talked to her. When I walked in, he was yelling at some little nigga that we had just hired. I didn't know too much about the little nigga, but something about him didn't sit well with me.

"So you mean to tell me that you just gave my shit to a nigga that you didn't know?" I heard my brother say.

"He said that you sent him," the little nigga admitted. I could tell by the way that my brother was looking that he was getting ready to kill lil dude. Just as the thought left my mind, he pulled out his gun and sent one bullet through the lil nigga's head. He dropped to the floor, I just shook my head and went to my office. I need to check and make sure that all of the drops and pick-ups for the week were in order. I didn't need shit else going wrong. I had a route that was set to go to Cali, and I needed shit to be smooth. It was the first time that I had shit moving out that way. I was sending three kilos of pure cocaine, I need that shit to get there with no issues. If it made there safe and sound, then that would mean that I was countrywide.

"Nigga what yo ass thinking about?" my bother asked as he and Gram walked in my office.

"This damn shipment. I damn near want to drive the shit myself," I said. They both just looked at me like I was crazy. I knew that I was overthinking it, but it was how I felt. It was always like this when I was going to a new state. I knew how I felt about a nigga playing with my shit, so I didn't want to play with nobody else shit.

"Gone drive yo dumb ass down there then superman. Yo ass don't like driving home but you gone drive to Cali," Gram said causing Jabo to laugh. That nigga was always trying to be funny. I just looked at them because they knew that I was dead ass serious.

"Damn I meant to ask you had you talked to Dea. I called her, and she didn't answer. I stayed at the condo yesterday," I asked Jabo changing the subject. I wanted to fuck this bitch that I met, and I knew that I could take her home, so I had to take her there.

"Nah I been with Erin. Let me call her," Jabo said pulling out his phone. He called her and didn't get an answer either. I pulled out my phone and tracked her car. It said that it was at home. I shut down the computer and headed out. I didn't need to tell them where I was going because they already knew. I wasted no time getting home. When I pulled in the gate, her car was there, so I headed in. When I walked in the door, I could have died. There was shit everywhere. It looked like a tornado had run through my shit.

"Dae, Deaja," I yelled as I made my way through the house. Everyone went their separate ways looking for her. I headed straight for her room, but she wasn't there. As was walking out of her room and something caught my attention. Her purse and keys were still on her nightstand. I walked over and seen her phone was there as well. I started moving shit around just to make sure that she wasn't under anything. I sat on her bed so that I could get my thoughts together. Jabo walked in, and he had this worried look on his face. I knew that meant that he didn't see her anywhere in the house. Shortly after Gram walked in the room. They both just stood there. Gram walked to her closet. I knew that he was checking to see if her gun was still there. When he came out empty handed I knew that meant that it was gone.

I got up and headed to my office. I entered the code and walked in. I cut the cameras on soon as I sat down. Both my brother and Gram walked behind me so that they could watch as well. I watch as a nigga disrespected my sister and my home. I studied the nigga's face trying to figure out how I knew him, but I had ever seen that nigga before.

"Do yall know that nigga?" I asked. They both shook their heads. Gram was on his phone and Jabo was looking at the screen as if he was trying to figure out something.

"I just sent the picture to my guy as well as the tags. We are going to find her," Gram assured me. I just dropped my head into my hands. I was her big brother I was supposed to protect her. I failed. I pulled my phone out and called Allia. I hadn't talked to her since the day at the club, but I was sure that my sister had.

"Hello," her sweet voice sang in to the phone. I held the phone for a second to take in her voice.

"Hey, have you talked to Dea?" I asked. I prayed that she had because I was going crazy at this point. I didn't want to have to call my parents and tell them that she was missing.

"Yea earlier why what's up?" she asked.

"I need you to come to my house," was all I could say. I didn't want to tell her what was going on over the phone.

"Ok." When she hung up, I laid the phone down and looked at my brother. He called Erin and told her to come as well. They were the closest people to her.

"Do you think we need to call dad?" Jabo asked. I shook my head and dialed my father's number. I put it on speaker. I knew that he was about to flip. I was mentally preparing myself for it.

"Hey son," he answered. He sounded excited as always.

"Dad I need yall to come home," I told him. I looked at Jabo, and he nodded letting me know that he seen where I was going with this. I could tell him over the phone just like I couldn't tell Allia.

"Ok," was all that he said. I knew that he could hear the sadness in my voice. I was just happy that he didn't ask what was going on because I didn't want to have to explain. Once we ended the call, I called the housekeeper and told her to come over because I didn't want them to see the house like this. Jabo walked out of the room, and I rewind the tape so that I could see if something stood out to me. As I watched the tape, I thought about all the shit that had been happening. I could help but to think about the fact that it was all connected. I need to find out who these niggas were asap.

19
———————

JABO

I walked into my sister's room and just stood at the door. There was no way that something like this had happened. My mind went straight to whatever nigga that she had been talking to. I remember the night that we went out she said that he went to school with her, but that was about it. Her phone began lighting up, so I grabbed it. It was Allia calling I just let it ring because I knew if I answered that she was going to start asking questions. I headed out of her room and back to my brother's office. Just as I was walking in, I heard the door open. I grabbed my gun and walked to the front. Gram was doing the same but coming from the other side of the house.

When we saw that it was Allia and Erin we put our guns up. Allia was looking around as if she was trying to see what was going on. Just as she was about to ask what was going on, Dub walked in the room. His face matched mines. I don't know if I was mad because I didn't know where she was or if I was hurt because I didn't protect her. She was my baby sister, and I was supposed to make sure that she was good.

"What's going on? Erin asked.

"Something happened to Deaja. When we got here, the

house was like this, and she is missing. Do yall know anything about the nigga that she was talking to?" I asked. Dub looked at me like I was crazy. I knew that he was finna shoot off, but it wasn't the time for that. I didn't know if it was the nigga that she was talking to, but I wanted to look at every option.

"What nigga she was talking? So everybody knew but me," Dub yelled. I just looked at him because if I had answered I knew that we would have been arguing.

"That's beside the point. I'm still stuck on her being missing. I talked to her earlier, and she was good," Allia said. She looked like she was about to cry. I hated to see her like that. I looked at Erin, and she was just staring into space.

"She was ok. I promise she was good," Allia cried. Dub walked over and grabbed her as she dropped to the floor. I was shocked to see him catering to her.

"Where is her phone?" Erin asked. I handed it to her. She unlocked it. She scrolled through Daeja phone as if she was looking for something. When she found what she was looking for she handed me the phone. It was a picture of her and the nigga. That means that whoever he has had this shit planned out. She had been around this nigga a lot based on the pictures on her phone. I sat there thinking about the fact that I had let that shit slide. I remember the day that we left the club she was supposed to tell me about whoever he was, and she changed the subject.

The whole room was silent as we all thought about what the fuck was going on. The doorbell rung causing us all to jump. I went to the door to see that it was the housekeeper. I let her in, and we all went to Dub's office.

"We need another spot before Pops them get here. We can't have mama and Jacey here," I told Dub soon as the door closed behind me.

"Yea call Brandon and have him to come over. I need yall to take care of finding us a spot. Just make sure it's nice and something that Dea would love. I want her to come home and be comfortable. In the meantime we can all go to the condo. It more than enough room," Dub reasoned.

"Let's get out of here. I don't want them niggas to come back and yall here," I explained. I didn't need shit else happening. We gathered everything that they needed then piled into Dub's truck. The ride to the condo was quiet. While riding, I noticed that a truck was behind us. I didn't know if someone was following us, but I wasn't going to take any chances.

"Aye, you see that truck?" I asked Dub. Soon as I said that everyone in the car looked back. He didn't say nothing he just nodded. Soon as he looked back at the road, he sped up. I looked and the truck was doing the same. Dub hit corner after corner until we made it to alley. He sat there until they passed us. Once he made sure that they were gone, we left for the condo. It didn't take us any time since we weren't far.. We all got settled while Dub went straight to his office that he had set up here. Everyone was just chilling here. The TV was off, and no one was talking. We all were just deep in thought.

"Let me see her phone," Gram said breaking the silence. I pulled it out of my pocket and handed it to him. He told Erin to unlock it then scrolled through it. Once he stopped scrolling, he laid the phone down on the table before hitting the speaker button. The phone rang a few time then a male voice picked up.

"So I'm guessing yall looking for Daeja well she with a real nigga right now. Y'all can get her back when yall hand over yall empire. Other than that I hope y'all told y'all mom to get her all black ready," the nigga said. Before Gram had a chance to say anything the nigga hung up. Whoever the nigga was had to know some shit about us because there weren't many people that knew we still sold drugs. We made sure of that. That was one of the reasons that we didn't have to worry about the police. I got up and walked out of the room because I was going to spazz. Allia and Erin both were crying and that shit fucked with me. I punched the wall so hard that my fist went through. I looked at Gram and I saw something in his eyes. I just couldn't tell you what that was. I wished that he wouldn't have done that in front of them. I didn't need them to be any more worried than they already were. I think that we all were still in shock from the call because the room was silent.

The only thing that I could think about was if she was ok. I needed to find my sister and fast. I knew that Dub was not going to play by the nigga's rules and neither was I. We had worked our asses off to get where we were, so there was no way that we were going to give that up. Hell, this was the business that my father had built. He had given to all of his time, and we weren't going to give it up that easy.

I text Brandon to see when he was coming. I need to get their mind off of all of the shit that was going on. I knew that all women like to shop so this would be good for them. Dub walked in the living room and sat next to Allia. She rubbed her hand down his back, and I thought that was so sweet. He laid his head back just as the doorbell rang. I grabbed my gun and walked to the door. I saw that it was Brandon, so I opened the door. Once I got comfortable we told him what was going on. Brandon was our cousin. His father and my father were broth-ers. Brandon grew up differently from us yet he was no different from us. If you looked at that nigga, you would think that he was a scary ass, pretty boy. His ass was a stone-cold killer. So I knew that they would be good around him. Once we told him what we were looking for they headed out. Once they were gone, it was just me, Dub, and Gram.

I looked at my brother, and he was looking at the wall. I was trying to read his face, but it was blank. I knew that he was thinking about how he was going to tell our father that his baby was missing. My dad loved all his kids, but Daeja was his baby. She was the reason that he got out that game. The day that she was born he said that he knew that he needed to change things. That was when he started teaching us all that he knew.

"Dad is going to flip," I said causing Gram and Dub to look at me.

"Yep," Gram said before walking out the room. He had been around long enough to know my father wasn't wrapped too tight.

"So neither one of them knew anything about the nigga that she was talking to?" Gram asked as he came back into the room with a bottle of water in his hand.

"Naw, they knew that she was talking to someone, but Daeja didn't tell them much."

"How the fuck did I let that shit get past me? I wonder if Sam knows who the nigga is?" Dub stated. I wish that I would have asked more questions when she told me that she was talking to someone but I didn't want her to feel like I was smothering her. Hell Dub did that enough for the both of us. He treated her like she was still in high school. Daeja was so sheltered. She wanted to be normal and we all knew that wasn't the way shit was in our world.

My phone started to ring, it was this female named Shenna that I had been messing with. She was a regular. I wanted to ignore her call, but I knew that she would keep calling. I knew that she wanted some dick but fucking was the last thing on my mind.

Yea," I answered.

"Hey baby I was just checking with you I haven't heard from you since yesterday," she said as if she was really concerned. All she was concerned about was me coming through dropping dick in her.

"I told you I got a girl stop fucking calling me," I told her. I knew that she was going to keep talking so I put an end to that before she had a chance by hanging up. I told her a while back that I had a girl, but she still called like I was joking. Hell I was happy that they were gone because Erin ass would have went off the deep end. I needed to clear my mind so I headed to my room so that I could get some weed to roll up.

When I made it back in the front Dub was gone. I headed straight for his office. I knew that's where he was. I walked in, and he was looking at the video again. He was playing the part where the nigga damn near dragged her out the house. There were tears puddling in his eyes. I knew then he was about to fuck some shit up, and I was going to be right beside him.

20

ALLIA

THE NEXT DAY

I had been at home for a few hours. I only came because I need to check the mail and get some clothes. I also wanted to have my car so that I could go to work. I sat on my couch wracking my brain thinking about what could have happened to Dea. I was going crazy, so I knew that her brother had to have been sick at this point. I was trying to think about if she had told me anything about him that could help them find her, but nothing was coming to mind.

A knock at my door pulled me from my thoughts. I got up from the couch and opened the door without asking who it was. Soon as I locked eyes with Cell, I wished that I would have looked before.

"What are you doing here?" I asked. He just smirked and pushed past me. The last thing that I needed was to have to deal with his ass. I knew that he was going to come and make things worse. I closed the door and walked back to where I was sitting on the couch. He walked around the house as if he was trying to see if anyone else was here.

"Again I'm going to ask. Why are you here? Don't you have a baby to be worried about?" I smartly asked. He stopped walking and looked at me. I knew then that shit was going to get ugly. He slowly walked over to me, so I was already bracing myself because I knew that he was finna start. Cell was one of those people that felt that the only way that he could get a message across was to put his hands on you. We had gone to blows plenty of times because he didn't know how to talk to me without using his hands. I was not one of those females that just let a nigga put his hands on me and not fight back.

"Cell do not come to my house with that shit. Go back to that bitch with all of that. I gave you so many chances just for you to go and get somebody else pregnant. Please just leave my house, or I will call the police," I said. I knew that would stop his ass because he was not trying to go to jail. He stood there looking to me for a second before walking to the door.

"Just know that you gone have to see me. Your mine and will always be mine. I guess because you fucking with that nigga you think that you can get away but you won't. I got something for the both of yall," he told me as he walked out the door. Once I made sure that he was gone, I locked the door and called Erin. I had to tell her about this. I wished that I would have listened to her when she told me that he wasn't worth my time years ago. I was just so dickmatized that I thought that I could change him. I saw the good in him. I knew that he could be a better person than he was, but he was too busy following up behind other niggas to see his own potential.

"Hey boo," Erin answered.

"Hey, you talked to Jabo?" I asked. I was so shocked that she had been messing with Jabo. Erin always said that after Eli that she would never be in a relationship again. She had held on to that word for the past four years. I could see it in her eyes that she was in love, but I knew that she would never admit that. After that night at the club, she told me all about Jabo. Once she did that so much started to add up. I knew that some nigga had been around by the small stuff that I seen at her house. There was an extra toothbrush, and some Gucci slides in her bathroom. I just didn't question it because I knew that she would tell me when she was ready.

"Girl he in the living room pacing the damn floor. He still hasn't heard from her. He just got back. I think they went up to the school to see if anybody knew the nigga. I'm trying to stay calm for him. I just went to get Eliza. She has been sleep since she got here, so they haven't met yet," she told me. I knew then that she was feeling him. Her ass didn't play about Eliza. A part of me could not believe that they had been talking all this time and he hadn't met her but then I thought about the fact that I was talking about Erin's ass.

"So how do you think that will go?" I asked. She didn't immediately reply which meant that she hadn't thought about that. We talked for a while longer until Eliza woke up. Once I got off the phone with her, I headed to take a shower. I had work in the morning, and I wanted to try and get some sleep although I knew that wasn't going to happen. When I stepped in the shower, I cut the water on hot and just let it rain down on my body. My mind drifted off to Daeja. I just prayed that she was ok. I needed her to be ok. She was like a little sister to me. After I washed up, I went to my room to find something to throw on. Just as I was pulling the clothes from my drawer my doorbell rang. I grabbed my robe and went to see who it was. I hoped that it wasn't Cell's ass again. If it was his ass, he was going to be out there knocking. I walked to the door and looked out of the peephole. Soon as I saw Dub's face, I ran to the mirror to make sure that I looked ok. I had no idea why I was doing that because I knew that I didn't need to be even looking at him like that. I love Daeja, and I didn't want to ruin our friendship.

I opened the door, and I swear my shit got wet. It was good

that I didn't have on any panties because they would have been soaked. "Ummm hey," I said after staring at him. He smirked so I knew that he liked the fact that he had me stuck.

"I just wanted to come by and check on you. You said that you were going to be an hour or so I just wanted to make sure that you was good. You didn't answer when I called," he said as he walked in. I just shut the door behind him. That nigga walked over and sat on my couch and kicked his feet up. I just stood there because he had lost his damn mind.

"Have you heard anything?" I asked. He shook his head no, and I flopped down on the couch and dropped my head in my hands. That's when it hit me. "Did yall check her GPS on her phone or in her car?" He looked at me as if something clicked in his head.

"Get dressed. I will be waiting in the car," was all that he said before getting up and walking out the door. I ran to my room. I grabbed the first thing that I could find which was some tights and an oversized white t-shirt. I slid my feet into my Jordan 12's, grabbed my purse and clothes that I had just packed. I locked the house up and headed to his car. Soon as my ass touched the seat, he pulled off. I didn't even have the time to adjust in the seat.

The whole ride to his house was quiet. I don't know how I didn't think about that at first. We pulled up at their home in no time. He went straight to the garage. I took that time to call Erin. It had been almost two hours since the last time that I had talked to her.

"Hello," she answered.

"Is everything ok?" I questioned. I prayed that it went good for her because Eliza was anti-social.

"Girl yes. She calmed him a little. They in the room playing tea party," she told me. I was so happy for her. I just hope that Jabo was good to her because she didn't need another Eli in her life.

"That's good boo. I'm with Dub," I told her. I knew that she was smiling because she swore that we were going to be together, but I knew that wasn't happening. I need to get past Cell before even thinking about messing with someone else. Just as I said that my other line beeped. I pulled the phone from I ear to see Cell's name displayed across the screen.

"This nigga just don't get it," I mumbled out.

"Who Cell?" she asked.

"Girl yes. He came by earlier and I put his ass out. Now he calling. I wish he would just tend to his baby mama and leave me alone," I said rolling my eyes as if she could see me. I could feel Dub looking at me.

"You know that nigga not gone let you go that easy," she reminded. I didn't reply because what she was saying was true. I also didn't want to say too much in front of him. Cell was not going to let go easily although I felt that he should have.

"Maybe I should lie and tell him that I'm pregnant that way he will leave me alone," I joked. Soon as the words left my mouth, I looked at him, and he raised an eyebrow. I don't know why my ass felt comfortable talking around his ass. I knew that he would probably try and murder my ass. Cell was crazy as hell. I looked at my phone again to see that he texted me.

Cell: so you got the nigga in my house
Me: one that's my house, not ours so with that being said I can
have who I want there

Cell: bet

"Girl now his ass texting asking about me having Dub in the house. I'm so over his ass. I know that I have accepted his shit in the past, but I'm not going to accept this period," I explained. Cell had a hold on me, and I was going to break it even if it killed me. He was my downfall. I allowed him to treat me any know of way and that was going to end. I could feel; Dub burning a hole in the side of my head. I knew that I needed to get off the phone with her before I said the wrong shit.

"Ima call you back," I told her before hanging up. The rest of the ride was quiet. I just kept taking glances at him. I didn't want him to know that I was looking at him. I didn't want to give him any ideas. When we got to the condo, we pulled into the garage. I looked at him, and I could see the pain in his eyes.

He got out of the car and then came to open the door for me. He grabbed me then we headed to the elevator. The whole ride up he was holding my hand. I felt so protected. When the elevator door opened, he stepped out first and lead me to the door. Once we were in the house, he just stood there and stared at me. I felt so shy under his gaze. He leaned in to kiss me just as the doorbell rang. He dropped his head before looking cutting the TV on so that he could see who was at the door. Whoever it was must have followed us because we had only been here five minutes. I could see the screen from where I was standing. It was a female. The way that he was looking I'm guessing that it was someone that he didn't want to see. He turned around then walked to the door. I followed behind because I wanted to be nosey. I took a seat on the couch and pulled out my phone.

"Roz what do you want?" he asked the girl.

"So you have been seeing me call your phone Dub and who the fuck is she. I know you haven't had her around my baby," she damn near yelled. I just took a seat on the couch.

"Yo Jacey is with my mom, so there is no reason for you to be calling me. And how did you know that I was here" he said as he blocked her from walking in the house.

"I just wanted to make sure that she was good and I followed you because when I got to the house, you were pulling off," she said sounding sad. Hell, I didn't know that he had a kid. I knew that Dae said that she had a niece, but I would have thought that Jabo was the one that had kids because she was always talking about how many women that he had. He talked to the girl for a while longer before she left mad. I tuned them out, so I had no idea what he had said to her. Once he closed the door, he walked over to where I was at sat next to me.

"My bad about that. That was my baby mama she be tripping but fuck her. Let's go in the office and enter the address in Maps so that we can see where it's at." I just followed him to the office.

"You familiar with this address," he asked as he typed it in. I had ever been to that address with her, but I was sure that it was the nigga's address because that was the last place that she went.

"Naw, but if that is the last place she was at, then that's not his place. When we talked last, she said that she was over there and that she felt uncomfortable. So I called and faked like something was wrong so that she could leave. We stayed on the phone till she got home. That's how I knew that she was at home and safe," I explained to him.

"Damn I wish that she would have called me. I'm happy that she did call someone though because there is no telling what would have happened to her there. I know I never had the chance to tell you but thanks for taking her under your wing. She is not good at picking friends at all. I'm just happy that God placed you and Erin in her life," he said causing me to smile. I guess he wasn't as bad as I thought that he was. If someone would have told me that this was the same man whose car that I ran into I would have thought that they were lying. I was slowly seeing the real Dub, and I can't lie and say that I wasn't loving it. He shut his laptop down, and we headed back to the living room. I sat on the couch, and he picked up his phone. Shortly after he started talking. I really wasn't listening to him because I was too stuck on the fact that Cell's baby mama posted a picture of them and tagged me in it. It was like she was picking with me for now reason. I hadn't done shit to her. She was the one that was cheating with my man. She was the home wrecker. In all honesty, I wasn't really mad at her because she had done me a favor. She gave me the push that I needed to leave his ass alone. I was so head over heels for his ass that I looked over all of the lies and cheating.

"You good? He asked pulling me from my thoughts. I got stuck looking in his eyes. I knew at that moment that I needed to keep my distance.

"Yes I just was thinking about Dea," I told him. He just nodded and pulled me closer. We sat on the couch and talked until Gram called. He went to his office, and I went to fix something to eat.

21

ERIN

I was so happy that Jabo and Eliza clicked. I just knew that she was going to be distant, but she wasn't. "You know you gone be my wife one day right?" he told me more so than asked me. I didn't reply. I just looked at him and smiled. A part of me wished that I would have given him a chance a long time ago, but at the same time in the back of my mind, I thought about all of the hoes that he had. That had been quiet for the most part, but I knew sooner or later they were going to come full force once people started finding out about us.

"You know that if you play with me, I'm going to kill yo ass," I said making him laugh. Baby, I wouldn't do that I been waiting too long for this to happen there is no way that I would fuck this up baby," he assured me. When he said that I kissed him causing him to start rubbing his hands down my legs. His hands were so soft. I loved the way that he gently rubbed my body. Just as he was pulling the covers off of me his phone rung. I got up and went to cut the shower on. I knew that he was going to be ready to shower and leave by his tone. I also could tell that he was talking to Dub. I prayed that he was calling to say that he had found Daeja.

"Baby we have to go. I'm going to take yall to the condo," he told me, and he stepped into the shower. I walked into the room so that I could get Liza together. I grabbed her overnight bag and packed her some clothes. Once I heard him cut the shower off, I grabbed her shoes

"Eliza put your shoes on," I instructed. She took her eyes away from the TV and did as I told her.

"Mommy where is my Jabo?' she asked. I just stood there because I didn't expect that.

"Umm, he is in the room. Get your shoes on we are going to go to his house for a few days," told her. She jumped up and down. I just smiled because she was only this excited to go to my parent's house. Hell, she wasn't this excited when it was time for her to come home. Once she had her shoes on, I headed to my room so that I could throw some clothes on. I also grabbed me some more clothes. Once we all were ready, I cut everything off and we headed out the door. He made sure that Eliza was good then he got in. He looked at me before pulling off. I had no idea what that was about, but I knew it wasn't the time to question him. I pulled my baby iPad out, put it on YouTube the handed it to her. I knew that would keep her distracted as always.

My phone started to ring, so I pulled it out of my purse. It was Eli, so I hit ignore. I knew that if I answered that he was going to hit me with twenty-one questions. Also, I didn't want shit else to make Jabo mad. Soon as I hit ignore his ass called right back. I looked at Jabo, praying that he wasn't paying attention.

"Answer for whoever that is Erin," he said letting me know that he heard my phone. Even though he said to answer, I wasn't crazy. That shit was going to backfire on my ass. He was in a fucked-up place, and I was not about to make shit worse. Soon as the phone stopped ringing, I powered it off. I knew that I shouldn't have been thinking like that because he wasn't my man, but it was how it was. The rest of the ride no one said a word. We pulled up to the condo, and we just sat there for second. I knew that he was finna say something crazy so I just waited. "Whoever that was you need to make sure that they don't call again," he said before getting out then getting Eliza. I didn't worry with saying shit because I knew that what he was saying was Bible and there was no need to go against what he was saying.

"I will get the bags just come on," Jabo told me as he walked towards the elevator. I just nodded and grabbed my purse and followed him. He and Eliza had a conversation on our way up, but I had no idea what they were saying because I was too busy watching how he was interacting with her. As a mother that's all that you want. A man that loves your child as much as he loved you. Hell her father didn't give her that much attention. The dinging of the elevator pulled me from my thoughts. We walked into the house. I loved this condo. It overlooked the city.

"Damn it smells good in here," Jabo said as he sat Eliza on the couch. I knew that it was Allia's ass cooking. Any time that she was worried she cooked. I sat my purse down and made my way to see what she was cooking up. I knew soon as Eliza found out that Allia was here she was going to be all over her. Just as I thought soon as Allia walked in the living room, Eliza ran straight to her.

"Tee Tee" Eliza exclaimed.

"Hey boo," she greeted Eliza with a smile. That was one of the things that I loved about Allia, she always had a smile on her face. With so much going on you would think that she would be spazzing out, but she was all smiles.

"Girl, what you in here cooking?" I asked. All of the stuff was covered as always. She hated people to see what she was cooking until she was done.

"You will see when I'm done."

"Did you make cake Tee Tee you know that I love your

cake," Eliza smiled." Just as I said that Jabo walked in and did the unthinkable. That nigga raised the top of one of her pots. She popped that nigga on the hand like he was five. I couldn't do shit but laugh.

"What was that for?" he questioned with his face frowned up.

"Don't go in my pots. Didn't yo mama teach you that," she fussed. I laughed so damn hard because he looked like he was shocked. Allia did not play that shit.

Dub walked in the room, and my eyes instantly went to Allia. It was like she was in a daze. I just shook my head because a part of me knew that she didn't need that in her life. Hell, she wasn't even over Cell's bitch ass. Now I could say that I was actually happy that she was even looking at someone else. They were looking at each other as if me and Jabo weren't in the room.

"Um hello, nigga we got shit to do you can stare on your own damn time. You need to be staring at yo car that she fucked up," Jabo said causing us all to look at him. His ass always had to be the one to say the wrong shit at the wrong time. Dub didn't say a word he just walked out the room. I looked at Allia, and she seemed to still be in a daze. She let Eliza down, and she ran back in the living room were her iPad was.

"Bitch let me find out," I said as I took a seat at the island. I hadn't ever seen her like that, not even with Cell.

"There is nothing to find out," she said with an attitude. I just laughed because I knew that she was feeling him by that action alone.

"We can eat in a minute," she told me changing the subject. I wasn't going to push the issue right now, but later I was going address it. I went to get Eliza while she was doing her finishing touches. I stood at the couch looking at my baby, and a smile appeared on my face; she was perfect. Her curly hair was all over her head, and she looked like she was getting some of the best sleep of her life.

"Why you looking at her like that?" Jabo asked scaring the hell out of me.

"I was just admiring her that's all. I know she's going to wake up as soon as I move that iPad," I said as I walked closer to her.

"Just leave it alone baby. You can feed her when she gets up," he told me. He grabbed the blanket that was on the other couch and laid it across her. I never seen him so caring and attentive. I walked back into the kitchen and sat down. Shortly after Jabo, Dub and Gram walked in. They all were dressed in black.

Gram was finna look in her pots, but Jabo stopped him. That shit was so funny.

"Don't leave this house for nothing. If someone knocks at the door go in the room that I showed you Allia," Dub said before grabbing a piece of bread. Jabo walked over and kissed me on the forehead before he and Gram walked out. Soon as they left, I looked at Allia. She had her back to me, but I knew that she could feel me looking at her. Her ass was falling for him. I could see it in her eyes.

"You want to tell me what's really going on?" I asked as I nodded my head towards the door. I powered my phone back on. I knew that Eli had been blowing my shit up.

"I think they know where she is. When I talked to her last, she was coming from seeing dude she said that she felt uncomfortable. So we looked at her GPS and found the last address where she went. So I think they are going to check there," she told me as she handed me a plate. I wasted no time digging in. The food was good as always.

"Girl how about Eli called when we were on the way here," I told her. She looked up from her plate with a shocked expression. I knew that Eli was going start some shit and I also knew that Jabo wasn't wrapped too tight I didn't need them beefing. Just as she was getting ready to say something my phone rung. It was Eli calling once again. I didn't really know if I wanted to answer or not. I didn't have time to argue with him. In his eyes, I was supposed to answer any time that he called. He has always felt that it was all about him. I really didn't think that he wanted me he just could deal with the thought of me fucking with someone else.

"And now his ass is calling again. I'm sure that he has been calling since I ignored his call on the way here," I expressed.

"Hello," I answered.

"Yo, what the fuck you doing you can't answer when I call Erin. You acting like you don't know that a nigga in jail," he damn near yelled. I had to pull the phone from my ear to make sure that I was talking to the right person. He was talking to me like he was my damn daddy. Hell, my daddy didn't even talk to me like that.

"Eli don't call my phone with that. I don't have to answer every time you call. You are not my nigga. I don't know how many times I have to tell you that," I fussed.

"Say no mo," was all he said before hanging up. I didn't care that his ass was mad; nobody told him to go to jail. That was all on him. Me and Allia sat at the table talking until Eliza got up. I fed her, and we headed to the back of the house. With so much going on we didn't know what to expect so we wanted to be as close to the hiding spot as we could be.

22

DAEJA

"So you think them niggas really gone go for that shit," I heard somebody asked. I was in a dark room alone, and the voices seemed like they were far back, but I could hear them clearly. The house was so quiet that I could hear everything that was going on. I had no idea how many days I had been here, but I was thinking that it was nearly three. The room that I was in didn't have windows, so it was hard to keep up. I was beating myself up because I fucking knew better. I should have seen the signs, but I didn't.

"That's his sister you know he gone do whatever we say to get her back. Once he gives us that shit we are gone be good we just gotta wait it out," the other guy said. There were three people here; one of them was Corry's. I wanted to yell out, but I didn't because I didn't want to be abused again. I was taking advantage of every moment that I could. I knew his voice but the other voice I had no idea who it belonged to. For the most part, there had been one guy here with me, and I didn't hear him so I was assuming he was gone. He was the one that stayed here with me at night, and he was the worst. He had damn near beaten my ass to death and sexually abused me so many time since I had been here that I lost count. He thought that I was going to give him information on my brother. He had to be out of his damn mind if he thought that. I would die before I did that shit to my brothers. The one thing that I knew was that I wasn't dying any time soon because whoever was in charge made sure of that. He was using me as his pawn. He knew that if they killed me, then they wouldn't get what they wanted.

"Corry you need to go in there and make her ass talk," the new voice said.

"Nah I can't do that," Corry replied. He was a coward he couldn't face me. He knew that leading me on was a fucked-up thing to do. I would have felt better if he would have just kidnapped my ass. Then to think Sam was the one that hooked us up so maybe she was in on this shit as well. I prayed that she wouldn't do no shit like this. I had been there for her more than anyone in her life. I hope she wouldn't do me dirty.

"Nigga why. Let find out yo ass fell for her. We talked about this before Sam hooked you up with her," the boss fussed. Corry didn't say a word I just heard the door slam.

"Yea that nigga is in love," the unknown guy said. That was bullshit. Corry didn't love me if he did then I wouldn't be in this room tied to a chair fighting for my life.

"What's good yall," the guy that had been here with me the whole time said.

"Shit tripping off Corry's in love ass," they all laughed. That was the last thing that I could hear. I'm guessing that they moved to another room because I couldn't hear them anymore. A while later I heard the door open, then footsteps walking towards the room that I was in. The door opened and there stood the man that played with my heart. If I could move, I would slap the shit out of him.

"I just wanted to say that I'm sorry," he lied. I just looked at his ass there was no way that he was sorry. If he were, he would have gotten me out of here.

"We both know that's a lie, Corry. You played me. I trusted you, and you took advantage of me. I will never forgive you for that," I told him. It hurt like hell to talk, but that needed to be said. He just walked out of the room. I heard the door slam again before the other men walked in the room. I guess they thought that I had escaped. Once they saw that I was still tied to the chair, they all walked out the room.

"Well, nigga we out. We will be back later we need to find this Cell nigga," I heard one of the niggas said. The house got quiet again, so I was assuming that they all walked outside. My mind then went to the name that he said that was Allia's boyfriend name. A few minutes later he came in the room. He just looked at me. I was more than sure that he was finna say some fucked up shit. So I just stared at his ugly ass. Now that I think about it that was probably the problem. He knew that he was ugly so he had to make everyone that looked better than him feel bad.

"So you ready to tell me what I need to know?" he asked. I didn't say a word. I knew that if I had said something, he would have killed me, and I wasn't ready to die. He walked over to me and slapped me. I had to do a double take at the kind of nigga that slaps someone and woman at that. I was starting to think that nigga had mommy issues or something. He was on the phone talking to some girl and was calling her all out of her name. Like he was going nonstop then got mad because she wasn't saying anything. Hell, I wouldn't have said shit either the way that he was yelling.

"That's still not going to make me tell you shit about my brothers," I said after spitting out the blood that had puddled in my mouth. Just as he was getting ready to hit me again his phone rung. He looked at the screen and started smiling. I had no idea who it was, but I was happy that they had called.

"When I get back you better be ready to talk, or yo ass gone be dead," he said before walking off. I knew that was a lie because whoever was in charge wasn't going for that. I don't think he knew that I could hear everything that went on. For this house to be so big, it was poorly made. The walls were thin as hell.

Just like right now I knew that whoever called was calling to have phone sex. I didn't think people still did that. The good thing was I knew that he was going to go to sleep like he did every time. I don't get how he was able to nut that many times.

I tried my best to adjust myself in the chair, but it was so damn uncomfortable. I wanted to try and scoot the chair to the corner because there was a table. He had left a knife on there earlier when he was eating an apple. I was in so much pain that it was killing me to just move my hands. I was doing my best to act as if it was bothering me, but my ass was ready to tap out. I just wished that my brother would walk through that door. I didn't know how much more I could take. I closed my eyes and prayed that someone would come and rescue me.

23

———

GRAM

We had been riding for damn near an hour. We were somewhere in Tipton County. There were no damn street lights or shit. Who the hell would live out here. I needed to see people. These houses were too damn spaced out of me.

"I'm still trying to figure out where she met this nigga at?" Dub said as we headed to the address that he found in her GPS. I had been hearing about this nigga, but I didn't think that they were that close. I had been keeping my ears to the streets trying to stay ahead of them. From my understanding, they have been here for a few months. One of the niggas owned a barbershop in the hood. I had a few youngins hanging around there hoping to see the nigga that owned it but had some other nigga running it for him. I had that nigga hit up a few weeks ago. I hadn't heard shit else about the nigga, so hopefully, he was gone.

This shit hit me hard. They thought that I was riding because they were my niggas. That was partially the truth. I was in love with Dae and had been for the past few years. I just knew that they would go crazy if they knew that. Daeja was their heart. I didn't want to ruin our friendship, so I just loved her from a distance.

The whole ride I was praying that she was good. If she wasn't, I was going to fuck shit up worse than I already had. I had been combing the streets looking for her. I had damn near demolished that damn shop. So I knew that whoever the owner was, was going to come looking for me and that's just what I wanted.

"I want to know the same thing," I added. Usually, when it came to her, nothing got past me, but this had.

The car got quiet for a while. I guess we all were in our thoughts. "This bitch," I mumbled. I had been messing with this female name Tasha. She was cool at first, but now she was being clingy as hell. I had been telling her for the past few days that I was busy, but she was constantly calling. I was starting to think that in her mind I was her nigga and that was the furthest thing from the truth. She was a simple fuck that lasted too damn long. Jabo told me that I was fucking up I should have listened.

"Nigga who you talking about? Jabo asked.

"This Tasha bitch. I'm starting to think that she delusional or something," I said as I hit ignore on her ass once again.

"I told you that bitch was crazy glad I dodged that shit," Jabo said causing me to laugh. He always had some crazy shit to say.

"Well, shit nigga he did tell you," Dub added. I powered my phone off just as we pulled on the street that the house was on. We parked down the street from the house and sat there for a while. Dub said that we need to scoop it out first. He was right them nigga probably was waiting on us. I said a small prayer before we got out of the car.

"I'm going to go to the front. G you go to the back and Jabo you go in that side door. Be careful and make sure that yall watching yall backs," Dub instructed. We split up and went our separate ways. When I made it to the back door, it was open which was weird since they were holding someone hostage. The house was dark as hell. When I walked in, I stood there for a second so that I could see if I could hear anyone. It was quiet which made me worry. I knew that they couldn't be that damn dumb to leave her here alone. I made my way through the house making as little noise as possible. I knew that Dub and Jabo probably were doing the same thing because it was silent. I slowly opened the first door that I made it to. The room was dark as hell. I switched the light on to see that I was just in an empty room. I cut the lights out and closed the door back. If someone did come, I didn't want to alert them that we were here. I made my way to the next room. This time I didn't walk straight in I put my ear to the door. I was quiet, but I could hear a little movement. I slowly opened the door, and there she was. So I ran straight to her.

"We here Daeja," I assured her as I untied her. I damn near couldn't look at her because her face was so beat up. She looked as if she was barely holding on. She was mumbling something, but I had no idea what she was saying. Just as I was picking her up. I felt a presence behind me. At first, I thought that it was Jabo or Dub.

"I wouldn't do that if I was you," I heard a voice say. The room was kind of dark so I really couldn't see the person. I went for my gun, but I wasn't moving fast enough because I felt a bullet pierce through my arm. That didn't stop me though. I let off three shots. I knew that I hit him at least once. I looked at Daeja to make sure that she was good.

"What the fuck," I heard Dub yell as he walked in the room and found the light switch. The nigga that shot me was laying in the floor with a bullet in his head. Dub ran over to Daeja. He picked her up as Jabo was walking in he helped me up and we headed out the same way that we came in. Soon as we made it to the car, we saw three cars pull up. What they didn't know was that they were too late. Dub pulled off and the more that he drove, the weaker I felt.

"Nigga hell naw you better stay yo ass up," was the last thing that I heard Jabo say before I blacked out.

24

FOUR

Jabo

"This nigga," I sighed in frustration. We had gotten my sister back, and this nigga was trying to die on me. I couldn't see where we had been shot because there was so much blood. He was wearing a white shirt, so it looked bad.

"Hold on nigga we almost there," Dub begged. Gram was like a brother, so If I lost him, I was going to be fucked up. I had already called the family doctor and told him to meet us at the house. I was happy that we found her because if my father would have gotten here and she was still missing, he was going to flip. Now we just had to hear his mouth about not watching her. What he needed to see was that she was grown and we couldn't watch her every move. When we pulled out the driveway. I jumped out to help Gram and Dub helped Deaja.

Soon as we walked in, he immediately started working on Gram. I went to find Erin and Allia. I walked all around the house but I didn't see them. My phone rung and I just shook my head. It was like these females didn't understand English. I was not about to fuck up with Erin. I made a mental note to get my number changed. I didn't need the drama. Erin was all that I wanted.

"Baby, it's us come to the front but don't bring baby girl," I told her. Five minutes later they came in the living room. Deaja was laid out on the couch. They both ran to her. I knew that would make sure that she was good while the doctor took care of Gram. Dub was standing at the door looking worried.

"He gone be good," I assured him. Gram was a hard body so I knew that he was going to pull through, plus he was only shot in the arm so he would be ok. It was just a lot of blood.

The front door opened and I grabbed my gun. I looked up to see my father. Lucky for us my niece was sleep. My mom walked past us straight to the back without saying a word. I knew that she was going to come right back because she saw Deaja.

"What's going on?" my father asked. I motioned for him to follow me in the kitchen. I explained everything to him, and he was furious. Just like I knew that he would be. Once he gained his composure, he headed back in the living room. I stayed in the kitchen because I needed to get some shit together to get us all out of this house asap. I knew that them niggas were coming; it was no doubt about that. I called Brandon to check and see how shit was going with the house that they found. He said that he found some shit that we would really like.

"Ma you ok ?" I asked soon as I walked in the room. She had her back to me, but I knew that she was crying. That shit fucked me up. I never wanted to see her hurt.

"I just hate that yall have to live this life," she confessed. I knew how my mom felt about the life that we lived. She had told us that so many times. I didn't know what to say to her at this point because there was no turning back. I just walked out of the room. When I got back in the living room, the doctor was looking at Daeja. She was up, but her eyes were swollen so you couldn't really tell. The room was quiet; the only thing that could be heard was Allia's whimpers.

Once we made sure they were good me, my brother and my father headed to the old house. There were a few things that we needed to get. When we pulled up, Dub got out first, and then I got out and headed to the back of the house. I didn't know nothing about these niggas, so I wanted to make sure they weren't here. Shortly after we walked in the house, my father walked in. I went to my room to grab some shit and Dub went to his office. I grabbed the bag that I packed and headed to my brother's office. While I waited, I texted to see if there was anything that Deaja needed. I got all of the stuff that she needed, and we headed out. As we walked to the car, I felt like I was being watched. I looked around, but didn't see anything that stuck out to me, so I didn't alert my brother or father. My father got in Daeja's truck, and we got in my car. I didn't know why I felt weird, but I didn't want my father to get caught up in our shit.

"Aye, when you get on the e-way don't go straight to the house. We were followed," I told Dub. He nodded and kept driving. I was looking out the side mirror as the truck sped up to stay behind us. Whoever these niggas were didn't know what they were doing.

"See I told you," I said making my brother look out of his mirror. He just smirked and sped up. The faster we went, the faster the car went. Dub jumped off the e-way and rode a few back streets just to make sure that we were right. When we got close to Grip's shop, I called him.

"Aye, you at the shop?" I asked soon as he answered.

"Yea."

"Open the gate. It's some nigga following us, so you know what to do," I told him. Just as we were pulling up the gate opened. I knew that they weren't going to run in here but I was sure that they would be waiting on us to come out.

"Yall found Dae?' he asked soon as we got out of the car.

"Yea she's with moms. We had to pop one of them niggas. That's them following us," I told him. We all walked to his office and just as I thought they were sitting there waiting for us. Little did they know we had some shit for they ass. See Grip was a mechanic by day and a hit man by night. He was dead ass like a thief in the night. He walked out of the office, so I knew what was up. We just sat there and watched it all play out. Grip slipped up behind them, and they didn't know what hit them. The nigga murked both of the niggas with one shot a piece. Soon as he walked back in the building, some nigga was pulling up getting the niggas out the car. Once that was done we got back in the car and headed out. I knew that this shit still wasn't over but at least we could chill for the night. I wanted to be under my girl and get some sleep.

25

FIVE

Allia
A FEW DAYS LATER

Since they had found Dae and Gram was good, I had Dub to bring me home because I had to go to work and didn't have any work clothes at the condo. I knew that I was more than likely fired from the hotel because I hadn't been there since the night that I met his ass at the club. Just as I was getting ready to shower my doorbell rang. I told Dub's ass that I need an hour hell he had just left. I made my way to the door. Soon as I got to it, I swung it open. Once again my ass should have looked.

"So you really want to play with me Allia," Cell said as he pushed his way in my house. I couldn't understand how he didn't get that I was done with his ass.

"Cell I told you that we are done. I can't keep doing this with you," I damn near cried. I really loved this nigga. I stuck with his ass through all kinds of shit just for him to get someone else pregnant. "I would move a fucking mountain for you Cell. I stole for you. I did all kinds of shit just for you to do that to me. Then you took my money like you was paying the rent and you wasn't. If it weren't for Erin my ass would be living on the fucking street," I cried. At that point, I was crying so hard that I damn near couldn't stand. As much as I acted like it didn't matter to me, it did. I was heartbroken and angry.

"Look baby I didn't mean for that to happen. Just let a nigga back in. I promise that I don't want her. She was just a fuck," he lied. I wanted to believe him. Hell, the old me would have, but the new name knew that I deserved better. I needed someone that would love me right.

"Can you just leave Cell?" I requested. He gave me that look that always pulled me back in before walking out the door. I knew that he was going to come back. I just need to make sure that I wasn't here when he did.

I was getting ready to close the door when he stuck his foot in. Do the nigga that just left have something to do with it?" he asked choking me. I didn't know that he saw Dub leave.

"No."

"I will be back. I know that you just need time but know that if I catch that nigga in here you and him are dead," That was all he said before walking off. Soon as I closed the door, I broke down how was I being punished for him fucking up. I wasn't the one that had a baby on him. I don't think he get how he has hurt me. I knew that expecting him to see that was too farfetched. He was too selfish for that. Life was all about him.

I grabbed my phone and called Dub. I didn't want to pull him to the bullshit that I had going on with Cell. I would be able to live with myself if some got hurt because of me.

"You ready already?' he asked soon as he answered.

"Naw I was calling to tell you that I was going just drive myself to work. I will just come to your house when I get off," I lied. I had no plans of going anywhere him. I knew what Cell was capable of. That nigga was crazy, and Dub had more than enough going on in his life. I knew that he was going to protest, so I ended the call before he had a chance to object. Soon as I hung up, I headed to finish getting dressed. Once I was dressed I call Erin. I knew that she was going to be calling me.

"Bestie, what are you doing?" I asked soon as she answered.

"Nothing laying here. Eliza gone to church with Jabo's mom, and he gone, so I'm just chilling," she told me. I was so happy for her. I just hoped that she didn't let Eli's ass get out and ruin what she got going on with Jabo.

"Girl how about Cell ass done popped up again. He talking reckless so I told Dub not to come and get me. I don't want to put him in my shit," I explained.

"How is Deaja doing?" I asked changing the subject.

"She good she with her mom as well," she told me. I was happy to hear that she was doing better. I was beyond scared when she was gone. Me and Erin talked until it was time for me to go. I gathered all of my stuff and headed out the door. Soon as I walked outside, I checked my mail. I opened the light bill and dropped my head. It was well over four hundred dollars. Now that I was down to one job I need to figure out how I was going to pay for everything. I was not going to ask Cell that was for sure. I made a mental note to call them tomorrow so that I could make payment arrangements. I just need to shake this nigga he was no good for me.

I wanted better for myself. I wanted a man that had eyes for me and me only. I wanted to be happy. Be in love with someone that was in love with me.

26

CELL

I don't know why Allia thought that I was playing with her. She was mine, and that was that. She knew what was up. I jumped in my ride and headed to my baby mama's house so that I could make sure that she was good before going to meet up with my nigga. I also need to get my pain meds. I needed to have my ass at home laying down, but there was too much going on for me to be doing that. I was doing my best to deal with the pain, but it was slowing bring me down. I had been popping pills every chance that I got. I was taking them so much my body was getting immune to them, so they weren't helping me. Then I had been drinking and smoking every chance I got so that wasn't helping either.

That was one of the reason that I needed Allia back. I knew that she would take care of me and make sure that I was doing what the doctor said. Tia, on the other hand, was so busy worrying about if I still wanted Allia to make sure that I was good. It's like that was all that she cared about.

When I pulled up to the house I saw that her mom was here. That shit made me want to turn around. I sat in the car for a second and then decided to go back to Allia's house. I pulled off before the realized I was outside. On the way to her house I called my nigga to see if he had any pills. Once he told me he did, I made a detour to his house. It took me no time to get there. I slowly got out and headed to his door.

"Damn nigga I didn't think yo ass would be out in the street this fast," Dee said soon as he opened the door.

"You know they can't keep a real nigga down," I said as I shook his hand. I made my way in and took a seat. I was happy as hell to be sitting back down. I pulled out my phone and called Allia. She didn't answer, so I knew that she was ignoring me. I was going to put an end to that as soon as I left here.

"So yall know when the shop gone be back open," Dee asked.

Some nigga had come to the shop and damn near burned that motherfucker down. I was happy that no one was there when it happened. That was what I had to go and meet with my niggas about. I didn't really know what was going on because my ass had been laid up in the hospital.

"Nah," was the only reply that I had for his nosey ass. He handed me the Percs, and I headed out the door. I needed to lay down before my ass fell out. I made it to Allia's house just as she was getting in her car. I parked behind her. She wasn't going anywhere because I needed her to take care of me.

"Cell move your car. I have to go to work," she said as if I cared.

"Nah I'm hurting I need you to take care of me," I told her walking to the door. When I made it to the door, I didn't feel her presence behind me, so I turned around. She was standing at her car as if I didn't just say that I needed her to take care of me.

"Cell, I have to go to work."

"Allia don't piss me off. Come and open this door so a nigga can lay down," I demanded. She started walking towards the door. Soon as she walked up, she unlocked the door and let me in. I walked straight to the room. I had a few hours to lay down, and I was going to do just that. Once I was in bed, I heard her on the phone with her job. She knew what needed to be done. It didn't take me any time to drift off to sleep.

I ROLLED over to see who in the hell was calling my damn phone while I was trying to sleep. I looked at the clock on the wall and jumped up. I was two hours late for my damn meeting. I looked at my phone to see that it was the nigga I was working for calling.

"Damn my bad I took some pain pills and fell asleep," I told him soon as I answered.

"Nigga you got twenty minutes. Don't make me come to you," he said before hanging up in my face. I got up and went to shower.

"Allia," I called out. She walked in the room a few minutes later looking like I was getting on her nerves. What she didn't know was that I didn't care.

"What?"

"I need you to go to the car and get my bag so you can change my bandages when I get out the shower," I told her. She rolled her eyes and walked off. I got in the shower and just let the hot water hit my body. I washed up and got out. I headed to the closet to find something to wear. Once I found something I sat down so she could fix a nigga up. She had my shit looking just like the hospital did just like I knew that she would.

"Thanks," I said as I got up to get dressed. She didn't say shit she just walked out the room. I looked at the time, and it had been well over twenty minutes, so I knew that I needed to get going.

"We need to talk when I get back," I told her as I made my way to the door.

"We don't have shit to talk about," she said as she got up to go in the kitchen. Allia loved to make me mad. I don't know why she was trying me today. Just as I was getting ready to go into the kitchen where she was my phone rung.

"Hello," I answered.

"I'm outside you got two seconds before I come in," he told me before hanging up. I just walked out the door. I would deal with her ass later.

"So I guess you think this shit is a game," Slim said soon as I walked out the door. This little ass nigga really thought that I was scared of his ass. I was simply playing my role.

"I was on the way. I had to wash my ass," I told him. Before I had a chance to brace myself his hand slammed in to my face. That made the third time that he had done that shit and it was starting to piss me off. He was acting like he didn't need me. I was the reason that he had the connections that he had here. No one was fucking with his ass.

"Nigga if I say twenty minutes that's just what I mean. Now that we have that out the way let's talk about the fact that yo bitch fucking with the Dub nigga and you didn't think that I needed to know," he said shocking me. I didn't plan to tell him that because I knew that he was going to want me to use her against him and that was not happening. I didn't even want her to know that I knew Dub.

"So were that bitch at?" he asked. He had lost his shit if he thought that I was going to give my bitch up. One thing that I knew about her is that she was loyal. That meant that if she was fucking with the nigga, she would never tell anyone anything about him.

"Nah she ain't here," I lied. He just nodded.

"Well since she fucking with that nigga I expect you to use that at your advantage and have her to set the nigga up. Or I can just kill the both of them. I heard that you actually love the hoe, so I know you don't want that to happen. You can use her or I will use you, either way, I want their nigga empire, and I expect for you to help me get it," he told me as if I was his flunky. This nigga had me fucked up, but I was going to play his game for now.

"Ok." I didn't really have much more to say to him. He thought that he had the upper hand, but that was the furthest thing from the truth. I was the only way that he could make moves. The rest of these niggas were loyal to Dub and Jabo. There was no way that he was going to get anyone else to work against them niggas.

"I need you at the spot at nine. Don't be late," was all he said before getting in the car and pulling off. Soon as he was gone, I headed in the house.

27

ALLIA

I stood at the window listening to the conversation that Cell was having with whoever this nigga was. The thing that stuck out to me was the fact that this nigga knew more about me than Cell did. When I saw the nigga getting in his car I ran to my room so he wouldn't know that I was listening. Cell was really into some shit. I knew that he was fucking with some new nigga, but I didn't think that it was this bad. I watched as he let a nigga punch him and didn't do shit about it. I can remember so many days that he beat my ass and he had just let a nigga treat him like a bitch. At that moment all the respect that I had for him was gone. I walked in my closet because I could hear him coming through the house.

"Allia, that nigga that you been around. You need to end that shit. Do you understand me?" I said as he jacked me up. My face was blank. I didn't need him to know that I was on to his ass. I need to get away from him. I knew just what I needed to do to make that happen. I grabbed him and pulled him closer to me. Once he was close, I pulled him in for a kiss. Cell was a sucker for some pussy. He let my shirt go, and that was all that I needed. I dropped to my knees and pulled down the joggers that he was wearing.

His dick was already hard, so I just took it into my mouth. I just needed him to think that shit was good with us so that I could get away from his ass. I was sucking his shit like never before.

"Shit," he moaned out. Even though I was doing this for my own reason but hearing him moan turned me on. That was one of the things that I was going to miss about him. He could fuck a bitch's lace front off.

"Damn I miss this shit," he moaned out. When he said that I pulled his dick out of my mouth and made my way to his balls. I took both of them in my mouth and made a gargling noise so that it would make them vibrate. I knew he loved that. Cell had some of the best sex I had had in my life. Hell, that's what had my ass taking all kinds of shit from him. He would cheat then when I find out he would come home and fuck me so good that I would forget about what he had done.

"Come here," he demanded. I got up and did as I was told. When I was face to face with him, he kissed me with so much passion that it made my knees go weak. He picked me up and sat me on the bed then kissed me again. As his hands made their way to my center causing me to moan out.

I love the way that he touched my body. It was like with every touch I wanted to forgive his ass, but I knew that I couldn't do that. He made is way on top of me. Once he was all the way on the bed, his dick was right at my entrance. He slowly slid in causing my eyes to roll in the back of my head. He was slow rotating his hips. That shit felt so fucking good.

"Damn I miss this pussy," he moaned out. He started to move faster, and I felt my nut coming. One thing that I will admit he could fuck a bitch good.

"Just like that baby," I coached.

"Shit baby don't do that," he moaned out. I was tightening

my pussy muscles around him. His eyes were rolling in the back of his head, so I knew that he was getting ready to nut. That was all that I needed. I knew that either his ass was going to be knocked out or he was going to think that he had made his way backing to my life. What he didn't know was this was going to be the last time that he entered me.

"I'm coming daddy come with me," I moaned out. His body stiffened up, so I knew that his body was following my commands. Soon as he released, he laid back on the bed. I kissed him and got up. I grabbed a towel and washed him off. When I walked back into the room, he was on his phone. He was smiling, so I knew that was probably his baby mama. I knew that shit for a fact. Seeing him smiling at his phone made me realize that my decision was the best. I need to get away from him before my ass ended up dead some damn where. I just hope that Dub would believe me.

All I needed was for Cell's ass to leave the house or to go some damn where. I knew that I wouldn't be able to sleep if I didn't let Dub know what was going on. I wanted to knock his ass out, but I knew that I had to play shit cool so that he would leave and think that we were good.

"Aye, I gotta go take care of some shit. I will be back," he told me as he put his clothes back on.

"Are you really coming back Cell?" I asked as if I really cared. He smiled then came over to kiss me. It took everything in me not to roll my eyes.

"Yea baby I'm coming. Have that pussy waiting on me," I smirked. What he didn't know was that I wasn't going to be here. I was going to make sure of that. He grabbed his gun and jewelry off the dresser and headed out. I took a shower to waste time. I wanted to make sure that his ass was gone. After he didn't come back after an hour, I grabbed my keys and headed to Erin's house.

28

DUB

I had no idea what was up with Allia. She was good when I dropped her off. I was supposed to go back and get her for work but she told me not to, and I haven't heard from her since. She didn't have to call me, but a nigga liked having her around. I would never admit that shit though. Since she was with the shit, I decide that I would slide through Bri's house. It had been a minute since I fucked her, so she was well over due. Just as I was getting on the e-way my phone rung. It was Roz and rubbed my hand down my face. I knew that she was calling with some bullshit.

"What's up Roz," I answered.

"I need you to come by for a second. Some mail came for you," she said. I knew that her ass was lying because I had moved damn near two years ago, so there was no reason for mail to be coming to her house for me/

"Aite," was my only reply. Her house was on the way to Bri's house so stopping by wouldn't be out the way. As I drove I thought about all the good times that me and Roz had. Hell, sometimes I wish that I could go back. I wanted my baby to grow up in a two-parent household. Roz just was on that partying shit, and she should have been being a mother.

It was like she didn't give a fuck about anything but hanging out. Since that was what she wanted that's what I gave her. Since I had a minute before getting to her house, I decided to call my brother to see what he was up to. We still had found the nigga that took my sister, so I need to check in and see what he and Gram found out.

"Yo," he answered.

"What's up nigga what you go going?" I asked.

"Shit at the crib." I pulled the phone from my face to make sure that I called the right nigga. Jabo's ass stayed in the street. If not that he was with some female.

"Aw, yea nigga you in love," I joked. I knew that he was going to get mad because he swore that he and Erin were just cool.

"Nigga find you someone to play with. I ain't in love we just cool," he said getting mad just like I knew that he would. I didn't get why he didn't just admit that he was in love with Erin's ass.

"Well if that's the case then I can hook her up with my nigga because he said that he been had his eye on her," I said just to see what he was going to say.

"When you hook them up make sure that nigga picks out what he wanna get buried in," he said before hanging up on my ass. I laughed so damn hard. I knew that was going to make his ass mad. I called back but he didn't answer. I then called Gram.

"What up nigga?" Gram damn near yelled when he answered. That nigga was way too damn happy for someone that got shot a few days ago. He was back up moving around but still.

"What yo happy ass doing?" I asked.

"Shit just brought yo mom and sister some pizza," he said. That was odd because my father was at the house.

"Umm," was all that I could say. "You heard anything?" I asked. Gram thinks I don't notice the way that he be looking at Dea. I saw that shit a while back I just didn't say shit.

"Nah the nigga done disappeared, but I know that he will come back out and when he does he's dead," Gram gritted. Gram was my eyes in the streets, and there was no doubt in my mind that he was going to find who was after us. We talked until I pulled up at Roz house. I told him that I was going to hit him back as I was getting out the car. I grabbed my strap and headed to the door. I knock on the door and waited on her to answer. I could have used my key, but I didn't know who she had in her house. I did my best to give her privacy.

When she opened the door, I had to wipe my eyes to be sure that I was seeing shit right. " I can come back later," I said getting ready to walk off the porch.

"No come in," she said in the sexiest voice. Roz knew what she was doing. She was fine as hell. She was wearing a see-through robe with nothing under it but a thong. She grabbed my hand and pulled me into the house. My dick was getting hard, but I knew that I didn't need to fuck her. If I did, I knew that she was going to get on that crazy shit.

"What you doing Roz?" I asked as I tried to make my way back to the door. This was all bad. She grabbed my hand pushed me one the couch. I knew at that moment that I had no control.

"I miss you, Dub. I know that you miss me too," she seductively said. I was doing my best to hold my composure but I couldn't. It's was something about her. That's why I stayed away from her ass. She dropped to her knees then unbuttoned my pants. I just laid my head back and let her take control. I was not expecting this shit at all. I really thought that she was going to be on some petty shit, but I was mistaken.

"Can we just give us one more try for our daughter's sake," she asked before sliding her mouth down on my dick. I wanted to say no, but she had a nigga stuck. She was doing this thing with her tongue, and all I could do was throw my head back. If she didn't really miss a nigga, she was sucking my dick like she did. She was massaging my balls at the same time just like I liked it. Damn, she knew just want a nigga needed it.

"Just like that baby," I moaned out. She looks at me straight in my eyes as she sucked my dick and that shit alone as lethal. That was some of that I'm going to make yo ass fall in love shit. "Suck that dick, Roz. Show me that you miss me," I demeaned. She did just what I was saying she sucked my shit until I nutted. Then she cleaned me up. I knew then that she wanted a nigga back because she didn't swallow at all. I wasn't complaining though. She then started back sucking my shit til I was back on hard. She reached over to the side table and grabbed the condom. She opened it and slid it down my dick.

"Come ride this dick. Let me see if you really miss a nigga."

She did as she was told and got straight to it. She slid down and moved her hips in a circular motion that shit was the business. It felt so damn good. She was doing all the work. I for sure knew her ass was going to be good and tired when we were done.

She was fucking me so good that I was considering getting back with her ratchet ass. "Just like that baby I'm finna nut," I alerted her. When I said that she started moving up and down my dick fast causing me to nut all in her. I knew that I was going to regret this but fuck it. Once we both were cleaned up, I sat on the bed and called her over to sit beside me.

"Look Roz you gone have to do better if you want me to even think about getting back with you. You need to be a better mother and get on your shit. I'm not saying that we back together but we can just go with the flow," I told her. She smiled big as hell as she hugged me.

I knew that this was probably a bad thing, but we would see.

29

NINE

Erin

I was sleeping good as hell until some damn body came banging on my door. I knew that it had to have been one of Eli's folks because anyone close to me knew better. I dragged myself out of bed and went to see who it was at my door. I was pissed because I had just gotten home. Hell, I was happy that Jabo let me come home. He and Dub had been holding us hostage, and I didn't have time for that. I wanted to be in my own damn bed. There was no doubt that whoever was at my door was going to get cursed out.

When I made it to the door, I slung it open. I was not expecting to see Allia there in tears. I grabbed her and pulled her in the house. I looked outside to make sure that nothing was out of place. I didn't see anything, so I closed the door and went to sit next to her on the couch. I looked at her for a minute to make sure that she was good physically.

"What's going on?" I asked. She looked up at me, and I could see that she was afraid.

"I should have just stayed at Dub and Jabo's house," She

cried. Ok, now I was lost because she was the one that was so ready to go. Hell, I would have been good there, but she said that she needed to get home. I knew that it was because of Cell, but I didn't say that to her. I wanted her to tell me before I assumed.

"What happened Allia?"

"He is cool with whoever took Deaja then he knows about Dub he thinks that I'm fucking him. He said that he was going to kill him. Erin I'm just going to stay with Cell so that he won't hurt Dub. I can't pull that man into my shit," she cried. I felt so bad for because I knew that he had to have really said some fucked up shit to her. I also knew that no matter what I said she was going to think what he said was the truth. I hated to see her like this because she was always the strong one and here she was on my couch crying her heart out.

"Just calm down. You may need to talk to Dub first because I'm sure that they were after him long before he found out that yall was around each other. I can call Jabo over, and we can talk about this," I assured her. I didn't want her making any decision before thinking it out. She nodded her head. Pulled my phone out of my robe pocket and called Jabo.

"What's up, baby." He answered.

"Um I need you and Dub to come to my house like right now.," I told him.

"Ok," was all that he said. I got up to make sure that the door was locked. He had a key, so I didn't have to let him in. I grabbed her, and we headed to my room. I didn't know if Cell had followed her here so I wanted to be as close to the back door as I could just in case we had to make a run for it. Cell was sneak, so there was no telling. When we got to my room, she climbed in the bed and turned her back to me. I went on my closet to find something to put on. I knew that if Jabo came in here with his brother and I wasn't dressed he would have a fit. That nigga acted like he was my damn daddy. I was starting to think that in his head I was his and that was not the case. Jabo had way too many hoes for me. Soon as I got dressed, I heard the loud sound of his Hell Cat pulling in the driveway. I looked out the window just be sure that it was him.

"They here," I told her so that she could get up. She nodded and made her way out the bed. On my way to the living room, I stopped and checked on my baby to make sure that she was still sleeping. I hate that I let her go to sleep so early because she was going to be up early as hell. Once I made sure that she was good I headed in the front where they were.

"So what's up," Dub questioned. I was standing at the door. That led me to think that he wasn't fucking with Allia's ass.

"Tell them Allia," I demanded. When I said that Dub walked over to the couch and sat down. We all were looking and waiting for her to start talking. She took a deep breath before talking.

"I called you and told you not to come back because my ex popped up and I didn't want to pull you into my shit. Little did I know that you already were. I heard him and some dude talking about you and me. He said he knew that I was fucking with you. He also said that he was going to kill us both," she explained. I looked at Jabo, and his jaw was jumping so I knew that meant that he was pissed. Dub ran his hand down his face then looked at Allia.

"So what is yo nigga's name," Jabo asked.

"Cell," she told him.

"Marcellus Clark," Dub quizzed. She nodded her head up and down letting him know that was Cell's name. I was surprised that they knew Cell because he wasn't in the streets as far as I knew. Dub let out an angry chuckle.

"Aye yall grab yall some shit. I know that yall don't want to but yall gone have to come to the house till we get this shit settled," Jabo said. I looked to Allia to see what she was going to say. When she nodded her head, I got up and went to get my baby dressed. It was like life was normal then out of nowhere shit changed. Hell in a minute my ass was going to be unemployed. Allia had already lost one for her jobs, and I was more than sure the people at the community center was going to get tired of her calling in soon. Hell, she hadn't been to work in over two weeks, and neither had I. I didn't want to keep dragging my baby around, so I called my mother and told her that I was going to drop her off. At least I knew that she would be safe until all of this was over.

It didn't take me long to pack a few things for her and me. Once I was done, I went to the closet and grabbed the bag that Allia always kept over here. When I walked down the stairs Eliza was laying on Jabo, they looked cute as ever, Hell I wished that he could have been her daddy because the one that she had didn't give a damn about her. Thinking of him I hadn't heard from him in a few days, so I knew that he was going to call soon. It was like no matter how many times I blocked his ass he would find a way to call. I just prayed that I wasn't around Jabo when he called.

"I'm ready," I confirmed. Dub came over and grabbed all of the bags that I had before walking out of the house. I made sure that everything was off before heading out behind them. Just as I was getting ready to walk out the door, I saw a phone on the couch. I grabbed it to see that it was Jabo's phone. There eight missed calls from the same number. I just locked the screen and headed out the door. Once I made it to the car I handed it to him. He had a look on his face that I wasn't used to seeing. It was the look of fear. I'm sure the thought that I had been through his phone, but I wasn't that type. No one was going to get hurt by that but me. I buckled in, and he pulled off. The whole ride he was taking glances at me. I knew that he was wondering what I was thinking but what he didn't know was that he didn't have any worries because I didn't look in his phone.

30

DEAJA

I was laying on the bed with my mom. We had come to their house since it was bigger than my brother's condo. I hadn't really said much to anyone, and I hadn't seen my brothers since the first day that I got back home. Hell, I hadn't even talked to my girls. I just didn't want to be bothered with anyone. I knew that they all were going to ask me what happened to me while I was there and that was not something that I wanted to talk about. Honestly, I just wanted to forget it all.

"What you want for dinner? I feel like cooking," my mom said pulling me out of my thoughts.

"Ummm let me see," I joked. "I some turkey necks, mac, and cheese, cabbage, corn on the cob, yam and cornbread," I told her. She just smiled and got out the bed.

"Anything for my baby girl," she assured me. I was excited because that was one of the things that I missed about my mom. She was the best cook ever to me. I hadn't met anyone that could cook better. I just wished that they would be home more. Since my dad retired, they were always traveling. Once she was gone, I decided to go and check on my dad. I hadn't really seen him either, mostly just passing by. I walked around the house until I found him he was in what I guess was going to be a man cave.

"Hey daddy," I announced myself as I walked in the room where he was. He smiled and got up. Soon as he made it to me, he hugged me, and that alone broke me down. I love my mom, but I was a daddy's baby. I was crying so hard that I felt like I couldn't breathe.

"Don't cry baby," he consoled me. Just hearing him say that made me feel so much better.

"Daddy why me?" I cried into his chest.

"I don't know baby but what you do need to know is that we are going to make that nigga pay for this," he promised. He just held me as I cried. That was all that I needed at that moment. What I was dreading was seeing Dub because I knew that I was going to be down again. Although my father was a phone call away, Dub had been like a father to me. I knew that he was going to be mad at me and I wasn't ready for that. Once I was good my father said that he was going outside to smoke, so I went to shower.

The whole time that I was in the shower all I could think about was the way that I felt when I was in Gram's arms. I knew that I shouldn't have been thinking about him in that way, but I was. It was just something I couldn't let go. Then to top it all off, he took a bullet for me. I didn't think my brother knew that dude was trying to hit me. He jumped in the way, and I was going to owe him forever for that.

Once I was done in the shower and dressed I headed to see if my mom needed help. As I was turning the corner to go downstairs, I bumped into Gram. I looked up, and our eyes met. I was in a daze. "Um excuse me," I managed to get out. He licked his lips, and I damn near kissed his fine ass. It seems that he was at our house all the damn time.

"You good," he said walking off. I watched him until he

disappeared into my father's office. I stood there for a second because I was debating on if I wanted to go and say something to him. He needed to be thanked for what he did for me. Since we had been here, he hadn't said much to me he mostly talked to my parents. Just as I was about to turn around the front door opened and in walked Jabo, Dub, Erin, and Allia. It was something about the look that was on Allia's face that bothered me, but I knew that whatever was going on she would tell me. I took off running down the stairs. I hugged Dub so tight. I think that caught him off guard because for a minute he didn't hug me back. When he did start hugging m, it was tight. Jabo joined in and that was it, I was crying like a baby.

Don't worry we got you," Dub whispered. He let me go then I turned to my girls. They both were crying. I hate that I was so distant with them. I just needed to get my thoughts together.

"Umm sorry that happened to you," Allia said as all three of us hugged. Just as I was getting ready to tell her that it was ok, Gram walked down the stairs and ruined the moment.

"What I miss," he said causing us all to look at him.

"Leave it to yo mop head ass to fuck up the moment," Jabo joked. Before Gram had a chance to reply my mom came out of the kitchen with the broom in her hand. Jabo wasn't looking, so she got his ass good. Why the fuck you doing all that damn cursing lil boy," she gritted while hitting him. We all were laughing so damn hard.

"Ok ma," he whined. He was always the one that got hit. He knew that she didn't play that. My mama was one of those mothers that beat yo ass right where you fucked up. I remember when we were kids, Jabo tried stealing a toy car from Kroger. She caught him putting it in her pocket, and she beat his ass right in the middle of the store.

"How you gone beat me for cussing, and you just said like ten cussing words?" he questioned. What did he do that for? He should have just taken that L because she hit his ass again before walking off. Once she was gone, he looked at us and got mad. Erin was standing there with her hand over mouth like she couldn't believe what had just happened.

"You ok baby," Erin asked him. I couldn't do shit but laugh. I needed that laugh. Him and Erin walked upstairs leaving the rest of us laughing.

I took a seat on the couch. I could feel Gram looking at me. I just hope Dub didn't see his ass. He sat next to me, Allia sat on the other side, and Dub sat in the chair. I looked at them, and something was off. I just didn't want to be the one to bring it up. I cut the TV on, and we all sat there until it was time for dinner.

31

GRAM

I was doing everything in my power not to look up from my plate. Daeja was sitting across from me looking good, even with the bruises on her face. On top of that, I didn't want Dub to see me looking at her. Now that she was up and moving around this was going to be my last day here. There was no way that I was going to ruin my friendship. I needed to stay away from her ass.

The food was good, but I couldn't enjoy it because I was too busy thinking about her. When she was gone, I felt lost, and there is no reason I should be feeling like that. "So what's up with yall," I asked Allia and Dub. They both looked at me like I was crazy. Allia looked at Mom, and she looked at Dub.

"Well," Jabo said putting them on the spot.

"Ummm," Allia hesitated. I knew that Dub was going to get my ass for that. I was just waiting. He was one of them people that waited until you forgot then sprang it on yo ass. I looked at Daeja, and she was looking at Dub.

"We cool," was all Dub said before looking back at his plate. I knew that he was mad, but I didn't care. The rest of dinner was filled with laughs. This was something that I wished that I had growing up. I didn't have shit but a crack head ass mama. Once dinner was done their parents went to sleep, so we all went to the basement to chill. I made sure that I sat as far as I could away from Dae. Once we all were seated Allia found a movie after she and Dub argued for almost twenty minutes. I pulled my phone out and opened Instagram.

I went straight at Daeja page. I normally didn't do that, but I wanted to see what she had been posting. I see that she hasn't posted in a while. That didn't stop me from liking old ass pictures. I looked up, and she was looking at her phone smiling. Soon as I locked my phone, I saw that she had done the same thing. Since she wasn't allowed to post on social media until we found that nigga, I knew that she wasn't going to post anything.

I got comfortable thinking about if I wanted to text her. She was still next to Dub, so I didn't want his ass seeing me texting her. I looked up because I felt her looking at me. Soon as our eyes locked Dub looked at me. I just dropped my dead and unlocked my phone so that I could see what was going on in the Facebook world. When I logged on, I had three messages. One was from this female named Taylor that I was fucking here and there and the other two was from new bitches. I messaged Taylor back sending her my number because I knew that I wasn't going to be on here long. As I was scrolling, I got a text I didn't look to see who it was I just kept scrolling. Once I was don, I checked the text that I had waiting.

Dae Dae: *I just wanted to say thank for saving me and taking a bullet for me*
Me: *You know I would do anything for you Daeja*

Soon as I sent the message I regretted it. Because Dub looked like he was looking at her phone. He didn't look my way, so I knew then that he hadn't. I hope that she took that just how I was saying it.

Taylor: what's up: Me: shit chilling with my fam

Taylor: ok hit me up later

After the movie went off, everyone went their separate ways. I kept checking my phone hoping that she would reply to me. When she went to her room, I had given up. I called Taylor so that I could get my rocks off. Hell, I needed to do something to stop thinking about Daeja's ass. Just as I was pulling my shoes, my text notification went off.

Dae Dae: and I will do anything for you

That shit gave a nigga butterflies. I sat there and debated if I really wanted to go now that she had replied back. I felt like I nigga that was in high school.

Me: I hear ya

I was so into my phone that I didn't hear Dub walk in the room. "Nigga who the fuck got you smiling like that?" he asked damn near scaring my ass. I had my back to him, so I cleared my screen before turning around.

"Nun of yo damn business nigga," I joked. He sat on the bed then pulled his phone out.

"We need to handle these niggas before this shit gets worse than it is. Now that we know that Allia's ex is in on this shit we have to keep her ass out the way. I don't want nothing to happen to her," he admitted. That had me looking at his ass crazy because when did he start caring so much. That was new to me.

"So you like her?" I asked. I just watched his face because

that was how I was going to be able to tell if his ass was lying. I knew him too damn well.

"Nah."

"You lying but ok. What's the plan?"

"I just called Dell. I got him following the Cell nigga to see if he can lead us to the big fish. We need to find out as much as we can on this nigga. We have a lot of shit going on, and there is no way that I'm going to let these niggas get in the way of that shit. Plus you know that we don't need Pops getting involved. The last shipment made it to Cali with no issues, and that alone will make us millionaires." I just listened to what the was saying. That shit opened my eyes like a motherfucker.

Dae Dae: meet me at the pool house
Me: Give me like 20 mins talking to Dub

Dae Dae: ok

I sat and talked with Dub's ass hoping that someone would text his ass or something because I was ready to see what she wanted. Once he was done talking, he told me that he was going to see his baby mama. I wanted to ask him what that was about, but I also needed to get to Deaja so I just made a mental note to ask his ass later.

Me: on my way

I walked around the house just to make sure that no one was watching me. Once it was clear, I headed to the pool house. When I walked in she was standing in the mirror. When she looked at me, she licked her lips causing me to smile. Deaja was so damn beautiful. I sat down on the couch. She walked over to me, and before I could stop her, she kissed me.

"Dae," I mumbled. I was not expecting that shit at all. I had to let it settle in my mind because she threw me off with that one.

"I just want to show you how thankful I am," she said looking in my eyes. As bad as I wanted to fuck her I couldn't. She deserved better. She had been through some shit in the past week that no one should go through. I would never take advantage of her like that. Besides that, I had too much respect for Dub and Jabo.

"Dae I know that, but we can't do that. If we gone do this shit we have to do it right. I can't go behind yo brother's backs like that," I explained. She looked so disappointed. I felt bad but I was a real nigga, and I didn't do shit like that. She would just have to be mad.

"Ok," was all she said before getting up and walking out. I rubbed my hand down my face before getting up and walking out. I needed to find a way to tell Dub how I felt because there was no way that I was not going to tell him. I wanted her and the only way that I could have her was if I got her brother's approval.

32

JABO

A WEEK LATER

Shit was starting to get back to normal now. Since we let the house go, I decided that I would get my own spot because I wanted Erin to move in with me. I just needed to find a way to ask her. I was headed to look at a house and I wanted her to come with me, so I was headed to her house. I also wanted to take her to dinner. I pulled up to her house and cut my engine off. Just as I was getting ready to walk up to the house and I noticed a car that was sitting on the side of the street. That same car was here the other day but it was down the street. I walked up to the door and as if she knew that I was coming she opened the door.

"Who drives that car?" I asked. She stepped out the door and looked at the car.

"My baby daddy cousin. He always has them watching my shit like him and me are together," she told me. I just nodded and walked in the door. She had the house smelling so damn good. What she didn't know was that I was going to use that as a reason for her to move in with me.

"Where baby girl?" I asked as I sat on the couch. I looked around and noticed how nicely it was decorated. I never really paid much attention until now.

"My mama just came and got her," she said as she straddled me. My dick instantly rocked up. It was like soon as she was close to me that shit happened and it didn't matter where we were at. The other day we were at her mom's house picking up baby girl, and the shit happened.

"I miss you, baby," she said as she kissed me again. There was no need for me to reply because she knew that I missed her fine ass. She climbed off me and grabbed my hand. She led me to the back of the house. By the time that we made it to the room, she was undressed. I loved when she did shit like that.

"Bring yo fine ass here," I demanded. She came over to me and dropped to her knees. We had sex several times, but she had yet to give me head. So I didn't know what to expect. She grabbed my dick with one hand and rubbed my balls with the other. That shit felt so damn good. I closed my eyes so that I could enjoy the feeling. When I felt her tongue moving my eye popped open fast as hell. I looked down, and she was looked in my eyes. That shit fucked me up. I was mesmerized.

"Shit E baby," slid off my lips before I could stop it. She was doing some unheard-of shit. A nigga's toes was curling and all. That shit blew my mind. She was making humming noises and that shit made my nut spill into her mouth. I was no good after that. I just wanted to sleep. What she didn't know was that she was moving in with me. It went from me looking for a house to us finding a house.

"I just wanted to make you feel good baby," she kissed me. I just smiled.

"Well get dressed because I'm finna do something to make you feel good," I told her as I headed to the shower. When I got out, she was dressed in some Nike tights and a fit Nike shirt with the vapor max that I had gotten her last week. I decide to wear the same shoe and Nike joggers and a plain white tee. Once we were good, we headed out. I had looked at a few houses on the internet.

"Where we going, baby?" I didn't reply; I just kept driving. She would see when we made it. I went the long way to the house so I that I could see what the neighborhood looked like.

"These houses are nice but they so close together," she said looking out the window. I just nodded. We pulled up to the house, and she just looked. I could tell that she wasn't impressed. I got out then helped her out. She didn't say a word as we walked up to the door. We walked in, and she just looked around.

"Whose house is this?" she asked. I pulled her close to me.

"Today we are looking for us a house," I said looking in her eyes. I wanted her to know how serious I was. She just looked at me. I was trying to read her face, but it was hard. She was just looking at me.

"So you really ready to take the next step?" she asked me.

"Yes, baby. A nigga loves you. I want you and only you. I just need you to trust me. I would never hurt you. I'm done with all the hoes I just want a family with you baby," I assured her. Erin was something special. I wanted her to be the one to take my last name and to give me kids.

"Well on that note I hate this house. The kitchen is small, so there is no need to keep looking at it," she noted. I just nodded, and we headed to the next one. We looked at houses all day. Just as we decide that we were giving up for the day my realtor called me and told me to meet her at a house. It was like twenty minutes from where we were. I headed there. Erin was mad because she was ready to eat.

The GPS said that I was almost there, but we were on a deserted street. It was nothing but fields on one side, and the other side was woods. As we drove, we came up on a gate. I entered the code that she gave me and drove up the long driveway. When I got to the middle, there was a fork in the road. I followed the sign that said the address that she had given me.

"Oh my God baby look at this house," Erin beamed. The house was big as hell. I pulled behind the realtor's car, and we got out of the car. Erin damn near ran up to the door. When we walked in, I looked at her face and knew this was the house for her. I just need to know who lived in the other house.

"Hello again. I know that y'all said that yall didn't want to look at any other houses, but I knew that she would love this one," she told us. Erin wasn't listening because she was busy looking around.

"So who lives in the other house on the property?" I asked as Erin walked up the stairs.

"Actually your brother just bought it this morning," she advised. I pulled out my phone to call his ass because he didn't tell me that he had bought a house.

"Yo," He answered.

"So when you was gone tell me you found a house," I asked like I was his girl or some shit. He just laughed.

"Nigga I didn't think that I had to check in with you," he laughed.

"Fuck you," I said before hanging up.

"Let me finish looking around and make sure it's what she wants," I told the realtor. She just walked off, and I went to find my baby. When I found her, she was in one of the rooms looking at the awesome view. I knew this was the house for her.

"I want it, baby. How much is this house? Can we afford it? How much will it be a month?" she quizzed.

"Don't worry about all of that baby. Just worry about how you going to decorate it," I kissed her. Once we were done looking around, we headed to find the realtor. Once we let her know that we wanted the house, she said that she was going to let the seller know and that she would call me in the morning.

My baby was smiling so big. As a man that was all that you

could ask for a happy woman. "So what about my house? Can I sell it?" She asked me. Hell, I didn't even know that she owned her house I thought that she was renting it.

"You don't have to if you don't want to. You can keep it and rent it out. That could be some extra money for you. Oh and you can call that job and tell them that you quit," I told her before pulling off.

I knew that she was hungry so I was headed straight to get her something to eat. Life was finally falling in line, and that was all that I could ask for.

33

ALLIA

A FEW WEEKS LATER

"Please, Allia?" Daeja begged. We were at her and Dub's new house. She was trying to get me to stay there until they cleared everything Cell, but I really wasn't with it. Dub did something to me that I couldn't explain. It was like when I was around him nothing else existed. I knew that soon I was going to give in to his ass and that was not what I needed right now. Plus I had already been here for a while, and I didn't want to overstay my welcome.

"I don't know. I think I'm going to go and get a hotel," I told her. She was looking so sad that I was starting to feel bad. She knew that I hated to see her look like that. I sat there thinking about it for a minute. I really didn't have much money so it would be good if I stayed here to save money. I was already down to one job and damn near was about to lose that one. It was crazy how shit changed so fast. Just a month ago my life was normal. I had the same routine every day. Now I didn't know if I was going or coming. I was trying to get over one nigga and try my best not to get under a new one. It was like no matter how much I tried avoiding his ass I couldn't. I would wait until I thought that he was gone before I would come out of the room, but I would still run into him.

"Why are you acting like you scared of Dub?" she asked catching me off guard. I just looked at her because she had lost her mind. I wasn't scared of him. I was just scared of the way that I knew that he would make me feel. I didn't need that, not right now.

"I'm not scared of him."

"Whatever you not leaving and that's that. As a matter of fact, you are moving in. There is no way that you can go back there. Even if they kill him his family knows where you live. Just please stay," she begged. I sat there and thought about what she was saying. All that she said was true. They would find me, and there was not telling what he had told them.

"I guess I can stay until I can get money to get a new place. I just need to make sure that I can get all of my stuff from the apartment."

"Don't worry about that," she told me as she smiled. We talked for a while longer then I headed to make me a sandwich. I prayed the whole way down the stairs I prayed that Dub wasn't in the house. I didn't want to see him. I guess God wasn't listening to my prayers because he was in the kitchen on his computer. I didn't say one word to his ass. I just walked over to the refrigerator. I pulled out everything I needed. Soon as I was got to the drawer to get a knife, he walked over. When he touched me, it was as if my breath got caught.

"So you not speaking today?" he asked. His smelled so damn good. As bad as I wanted to be hard around him I couldn't.

"Ummmm I thought that you were busy," I mumbled.

"Nah, I'm never too busy to stop and talk to you," he flirted me. He was so darn close that I could feel his breath on my neck. He didn't have to be that close to me to talk to me, but I wasn't telling him that. He just stood there for a second as if he was savoring the moment.

"What you making us?" he asked stepping back. I finally let out the breath that I didn't realize that I was holding.

"I'm making me a turkey sandwich," I said. I was looking at him out the side of my eye because he was beside me. I pulled out two slices of bread then opened the mayo and put it one slice of bread. Then I grabbed the turkey and cheese. Soon as I laid it on the bread he grabbed the sandwich.

"Thanks," was all he said before going back to his computer. I just stood there because I could believe that he had just taken my sandwich. He looked at me and blew a kiss before taking a bite. I just rolled my eyes and proceeded to fix me another sandwich. Once I was done, I stood at the counter eating. I couldn't help but look at his fine ass.

"If you take a picture it'll last longer," he said letting me know that he knew that I was looking at him. The crazy part was that he never looked up from the computer. I just smiled and walked off.

"Aye come here," he demanded. I stood there for a second before walking over to where he was sitting.

"What can I help you with?" I asked trying not to smile.

"So my sister told me that you are going to stay here."

"That was the plan unless you don't want me here."

"I don't care about you being here. I got a few rules though," he started. "Don't walk around half naked. Don't open the door for anyone. Everyone that needs to be in here has a key. Lastly, don't drink my Simply," he finished. I just looked at him because I knew that he was just trying to make conversation, and if he thought that I wasn't going drink his Simply then he was crazy that was my favorite.

"Is that all?" I asked as I got up. He just nodded and looked back at his computer. Soon as I got up, I could feel him looking at me. I made sure that I moved my hips a little more. When I made it to the room, I dropped on the bed like a high school girl. I was smiling so hard that my jaws were hurting.

34

DUB

I sat at my kitchen table trying to work, but I couldn't help but think about Allia's fine ass. I was working on a business proposal for a chicken spot that I was looking to open. I had a deadline, so I was trying to get it done. I was trying open as many businesses as I could to make sure that my baby was set for life. I was tired of the street shit. I wanted to sit back and enjoy my money.

"What you doing big head?" Dae said walking to the kitchen.

"Just working on some shit. What's up," I asked.

"Nothing I just wanted to talk to you about Allia. Dub don't run her away. You know that she likes you but she going through some shit. I want her to be happy. Also, I need you to get her stuff moved. She wanted to go back, but I don't want anything to happen to her," she voiced.

"I will make sure it gets done asap," I assured her. She knew that I was going to do whatever she asked me to do. I had on my poker face, but I was smiling on the inside at the thought of Allia being here. We talked until Roz called. Soon as I answered my sister got up and walked out. She couldn't stand Roz.

"What good baby?"

"Nothing I was calling to see if you was coming by or do you want me to come over there," she asked. I was finna tell her to come over, but I saw Allia walk pass the kitchen.

"Nah I will come through later," I told her before ending the call. I got up and went to the backyard where I knew that she was. When I walked back there she was lighting a blunt. Hell, I didn't even know that she smoked. I stood there and watched her as she smoked and scrolled on snapchat. Soon as she got ready to snap a picture, I moved so that I would be in the picture. She whipped her head around fast as hell.

"Damn I can't get in your picture," I joked. She was blushing so damn hard.

"I'm sure that yo baby mama wouldn't like that. I'm done with my days of beefing with hoe's over niggas," she told me as she passed me the blunt that she was smoking. I took it from her and then sat next to her. I could feel my phone vibrating, but I powered it off. I wanted to get to know her, and that was all that I was focused on.

"So tell me about you?"

"I'm sure that you know plenty about me. Your sister already told me that you did a background check on me," she stated.

"Nah that was Jabo," I told her. That nigga didn't even tell me that he did that shit till after the fact. We sat and talked for hours. By the time that we were done talking Jabo and Erin were walking in the back yard. I looked at my watch and seen that it was damn near midnight. I knew that Roz ass was probably mad as hell. I was happy that she didn't know where I lived.

"What yall back here doing? Let me find out," Erin asked causing us all to laugh. I looked at Allia, and she was blushing hard. I knew that she was going to make a nigga weak. She was so caring and thoughtful. A part of me wanted to be what she needed, but I had Roz. I had just told her that we could try and work shit out so there was no way that I could just stop fucking with her. That would bring too much drama in my life.

I powered my phone on and just as I thought Roz had been blowing me up. I also had a missed call from my mother. I decided to call her back first. I knew that it was probably my baby calling. She had been at their house since they'd been here.

"Hey daddy," she said soon as I answered.

"Hey, baby girl. What you doing?" I asked. My baby was always so happy. I missed her.

"Can you come get me daddy?" she asked.

"You know I will baby girl. I'm headed there now. Let me talk to granny," I told her. I could hear the phone moving around, so I knew that she was looking for my mom. When my mother got on the phone, I told her that I was headed to get my baby. I walked back outside; they were all laughing. I loved how calm things were for now. I let them know that I was going to get my baby girl. I grabbed my wallet and keys then headed out the door.

I got in the car and then called Roz. I knew that she was going to be mad, but she would be ok. "Damn I been calling you all damn day I thought you was coming over?" she fussed.

"I got busy," I told her. I wasn't lying because I really was busy. Talking to Allia made me realize what I was missing in life. I needed someone like Allia. Roz wasn't what I needed.

"Are you still coming baby," she whined. Roz was cool, but I knew that she just wanted to fuck with a nigga because she wanted the attention. She wanted to say that we were together. She wanted the status.

"Yea I will be that way in a minute," I told her. I hung up before she could say anything else. It took me no time to get to my mom's house. Once I had my baby, I headed to her mother's house.

I knocked as always. She came to the door with nothing on but a little ass shirt that barely covered her ass. She was smiling until she saw that Jacey was behind me. "Aw I didn't know that she was going to be with you,' she said before moving out the way so that we could walk in. Jacey went to her room, and I sat on the couch. I could tell that she was mad, but I didn't care. This was her first time seeing Jacey since she had gone with my parents to Florida.

"When did she get back?" she asked as she sat next to me. I sat there in shock because she didn't say a word to my baby. She acted like she hadn't just walked in the door. The longer I sat there a watched her on her phone the madder I got.

"I'm finna roll," I said getting up. Soon as I said that she jumped up.

"You going to call me when you drop her off," she stupidly said. I looked at her like she was crazy. That just fucked up all the progress that we had made. She didn't give a fuck about my baby. All that she told me was a lie. She just wanted to get a nigga under her spell.

"Yo you a fucked up person," I said walking to the back to get my baby girl. When we made it back to the front, she was looking stupid.

"Why you leaving?" she asked. Her ass was sitting there looking stupid.

"You didn't say not one word to Jacey when she walked in. Besides that, you looked like you was disappointed to see your own child. What kind of shit is that?" I asked. She was just looking at me like I was saying some crazy shit. I was done with her ass. This was it for me. I stood there to see if she was going to try and explain herself. When she didn't respond, I walked out the door.

Me: can you cook something real quick
Allia: it's after midnight

Me: I know I will explain when I get there. Just do this for me, please
Allia: ok

I just smiled because she was so damn sweet. I just wish that I could have had someone like her to be the mother for my child. "Daddy why you smiling? Jacey asked. I just looked at her. She was her father's child because she noticed every damn thing.

"I'm smiling because I have you baby girl. I have been missing you," I told her as we pulled to the gate that led to my house.

"Where we going, Daddy?" Jacey asked. I just looked over at her and smiled.

"This is our house." She was so happy. She sat up on her knees and looked at the house as we pulled up.

"Daddy I love it."

"You haven't even been in yet," I laughed. Seeing her happy was everything to me. My whole life was devoted to making sure that she was good and had the best life. Especially since I knew that her mother wasn't going to do it. I just don't get how a woman could be that way about her own child. My mother had always put us first. Hell, I heard her, and my father go at it plenty of days because she wanted to do something with us, but he had plans for them.

I got my baby out of the car, and we headed in the house. When we walked in, it smelled so damn good. I went straight to the kitchen. My baby followed behind me. When I walked in Allia was standing over the stove. She turned around, and when her eyes landed on Jacey, she had the biggest smile on her face. Jabo and Erin were still in the back yard. If I didn't know any better, I would think that they was back there fucking, but that wasn't my business, so I didn't think too much into it.

"Who is this beauty?" she asked as she made her way

towards us. It was crazy that she was happier to see my baby then her own mother was.

"Duh it's me Allia," Jacey said. She was so damn funny. "You must be daddy's girlfriend, now?" she asked catching us both off guard.

"No I am not Jacey," Allia laughed,

"What you cooking cause I'm hungry," Jacey said walking to the kitchen. I stood there watching them talk for a minute then head to see what my sister was doing.

35

ERIN

"Baby I think Dub can see us," I told Jabo, as he slow stroked me. I was on top, and he was fucking me from the bottom. We were in the pool chair. This nigga wanted pussy no matter where we were. One day we were at the mall he made my ass go in the dressing room in Macy's. My baby didn't care; he wanted it when we wanted, and I gave it to him when he wanted it. There was no way I was going to give him a reason to want to cheat.

"So," was all he said as he drilled me. It was like I was fall more in love with each stroke.

"Just like that baby. Daddy finna nut," he moaned out. I started moving fast, and before I knew it, he was releasing inside of me. I kissed him before climbing off him and going to the bathroom that was outside near the pool. Once I made sure that I was good, we headed in the house. It smelled so damn good. Allia wasn't in the kitchen, so I went to the stove to see what she had cooked. Soon as I was lifting the top, I heard her voice. "I will cut yo hand off," she said. I just put it down and took a seat. I looked over, and there was a little girl following her. I was more than sure it was Dub's daughter. She looked just like his ass. She climbed on the stool next to me and then looked me in the face.

"Where is Liza," she questioned looking past us as if she was going to be walking in alone. Her and Eliza clicked soon as they met. My baby asked about her ass all the time.

"Liza is with her granny I will go and get her tomorrow so that yall can play," I promised her.

"Uncle Bo," she yelled out soon as Jabo walked in the kitchen. She jumped down and ran straight to him. That was the cutest thing ever.

"What's good baby girl?" he said pulling a hundred dolor bill from his pocket and handing it to her. He laughed because he did that shit to Eliza as well. That damn girl had so much money in her bank.

"Thanks," was all she said before running off. Once she was gone Allia looked at us. I knew that she was finna say something crazy.

"Yall some nasty as people. Yall live two minutes away and yall choose to fuck in my back yard. I hope the mosquitos ate yall ass up," she fussed. I just laughed because she was really mad. That shit was funny. I wasn't going to say shit, but I wanted to make her mad.

"Well if you gone and give Dub some of that wet wet then yall could do the same thing," I said. Soon as the words left my mouth, he walked in. She looked like she wanted to kill me. Jabo was laughing so damn hard. Dub was just standing there looking at her to see if she was saying something. She just stormed off. I just shrugged and picked up a piece of bread. Shortly after she came back with baby girl and Dae was right behind her. As we were getting ready to eat there was a knock at the door. Dub got up to answer. When he came back, Gram was behind him. For some reason, my eyes went straight to

Dae. She was blushing. I guess she could feel me looking at her because soon as she turned to me, her smile dropped, and I nodded. I just wanted to let her know that I saw her. She knew that it was not a good idea. I didn't know if they were messing around or if she was crushing on him, but it was not a good idea either way.

"Damn yall didn't call and tell a nigga that yall was cooking," he said making him a plate. He sat across from Dae, and I knew that was not a good idea. Dub was beside her and Jabo was next to her.

"Uncle G you don't see me," Jacey said making us all laugh. That little girl was something else.

"Sorry baby," he said pulling a hundred dollar bill out of his pocket and giving it to her. She got up and ran out of the room. I was guessing that she was going to put it up.

"Damn can I be yall niece," Allia said as she sat down next to Dub.

"Nah baby all you got to do is say the word I will give you whatever," Dub spoke making everybody in the room look at Allia. I knew that she was thinking about what she wanted to say back. She had her head down, but I knew that she could feel us all looking at her.

"I'm good on that," was all that she said. I was stuck. Allia was the comeback queen. She always had some shit to say. He had shut her ass up. I could wait to make fun of her ass. Jacey came back to the table and started talking. She was just like Eliza. They even called each other cousins and all.

"So can yall go and get my cousin now because we need to play with the new dolls that my daddy got me and I can't open them without her," she told us.

"How about we go to sleep when we are done eating, and I will make sure that they go and get her. It's late, so you have to get your beauty rest," Allia told her. Allia was so good with kids.

I knew that whenever she became a mother, she was going to be the best at it.

"Ok," Jacey said. Dub was just staring at her. If I didn't know any better, I would have thought that nigga was in love. I just looked around the table and smile at all the love. This is what I wanted for my family.

36

CELL

"So yall telling me that yall let them find her," I asked Corry. They had gotten a meal ticket and let that shit go. These were some dumb ass niggas. Then they thought that they were going to come down here and take some shit. Dub and Jabo were too smart for them. Just like right now they were pacing the floor thinking of a way to get them back for killing they nigga when I was more than sure that Dub and Jabo were three steps ahead of them. I told them when they came down here that it wasn't going to be easy.

"I don't know how they found her," Corry said. I did my best not laugh because I had told him that the nigga's reach was far. They didn't want to listen. I had known them nigga all my life. I just sat back and let them talk because there was nothing for me to say. I was too busy worried about Allia's ass. She had gotten her number change and moved out of the apartment that we shared. I thought about going to her job, but I didn't want her to lose her job. That would just push her away, and that was not what I wanted to do. I was going to give her a few more days before I went to her job. She was going to talk to me no matter if she liked it or not.

Tia: don't forget about my appointment in the morning

She had texted me that shit at least three damn times today. She wasn't going to give me a damn chance to forget. I was so ready for her to have this damn baby because she was doing the most. Every time she called, it was something. I take care of business because she always called saying that she needed something. I hate that I even got her ass pregnant. That shit was a mistake.

Me: you don't have to keep telling me that damn

I knew that was going to piss her off, so that let me know that she wasn't going to text back. I focused back on them. They were now talking about robbing one of their spots. The Corry nigga said that he had been calling Dub's sister but her number was changed, He couldn't have thought that she was going to talk to his ass. He had to be crazy. Hell, I wouldn't want to talk to her ass. See he thought that she was weak minded. Her ass had been trained for this shit.

"I need to find out how to get in touch with her. I know I can get her to meet me," Corry said as if he was sure of that. I just shook my headed. This nigga was a real dumb.

"Aye where your girl at their friends and she fucking with Dub nigga. You can get her to set that nigga up," he recommended. I just looked at him because I had already told his ass that she had gotten her number changed on me.

"What I told you the other day?" I asked irritated. I was getting tired of his ass. He was acting like he was my damn daddy and I was older than him.

"Nigga who you talking to?" Corry said jumping in my face. I just laughed because he thought that he was scaring me. I was a grown ass man, and they were going to treat me as such.

"I'm talking to you. I told you that the other day just

because you asking again don't mean that the answer will change," I said. Before I knew it, he was pulling his gun out. I didn't flinch. That shit didn't scare me, especially since I had just gotten shot a month or so ago. Corry was just a flunky he did whatever slim said. He was simply a do boy.

"You think that's scaring me?" I asked. I knew that he wasn't bout that life. He was just showing out. He lowered his gun, and I giggled. I guess that pissed him off because the next thing I heard was a gunshot then everything went black.

37

ALLIA

A WEEK LATER

I was sleeping good as hell until my phone started ringing. I looked at my phone and seen that it was Erin ass calling. I knew her ass didn't want nothing. She just wanted to get on my nerves. Her ass was bored in that big ass house just like I was in this one. Most of the time Daeja was in her room, so it was just Jacey and me. She was my boo. I had grown to love that little girl so much. I didn't get how her mother could treat her the way that she does. I would never do my child like that. I loved kids, so I was happy to have her around. In the beginning, he thought that I didn't want her here, but I didn't mind.

"What," I answered.

"I'm at your door," she told me. I threw my legs off the bed then went to get my robe so that I could let her in. I walked out of the room and walked right into Dub. My eyes went straight to his chest. He didn't have on a shirt. Once again I was stuck. I just stood there looking at his fine ass. I guess I was looking good too because he was doing the same to me, except he was licking his lips. I loved when he did that.

"Allia is that my cuzin at the door" Jacey yelled out breaking the trance that Dub had me in.

"Here I come baby," I called out. I gave him one more glance before heading to the door. When I opened it, Erin and Eliza were standing there looking at me like I was crazy. I guess I took to long for them. I didn't say a word I just walked off. I needed to shower after how he had just turned me on. I headed straight upstairs because I knew they would make themselves at home.

"Come here," he demanded as I was walking in my room. Dub and I had the weirdest relationship. We kicked it all the time. He even took me on dates, but we had yet to make shit official. I didn't know if I wanted to do. One day he would be acting like I was his girl and the next he would walk past my ass like he didn't know me. He was the perfect man in my eyes. He was so handsome. He was loyal and a protector. Let's not talk about how thoughtful he was. Like the other day, he took my car and got it fixed from when I hit him. I didn't ask him to do that, but he did it with no question. To top all of that he was a great father. He made sure that Jacey was good at all times. His baby mama was dumb.

"What's up?" I said walking up to him. Soon as I was close to him, he pulled me in for kiss catching me off guard. That was the first time that he had done that. I stood there waiting for him to say something because I needed an explanation.

"Ummm what was that about?" I asked. He just looked at me before walking in his room and closing the door. I wanted to knock that damn door down, but I went to shower. What he didn't know was that he was going to explain. On the way back to my room I stopped in Dae's room. She was on the phone. I didn't know who she was talking t, but they had her ass in a zone. She didn't even notice that I was in the room.

"You crazy," she giggled.

"About you," the nigga said. I listened for a while longer

until I caught on to the voice. Her ass was talking to Gram. She knew that it was not a good idea. Dub's ass was going to go crazy. His best friend and little sister. That was a disaster waiting to happen. I didn't even let her know that I was in the room. I just went to my room. I was going to address it later when Dub wasn't home. I didn't want him to walk in on us talking. He was known for that shit.

I showered then headed down so that I could see what Erin and the girls were doing. They are still on the couch watching a movie. I made my way down the stairs so that I could spend some time with them. I rolled my eyes when I saw that they were watching *Sing* again. They watch that damn movie all damn day. As always before the movie was gone off, they were sleeping. Erin and Eliza headed home, and I picked Jacey up and took her to her room. Once I made sure that she was good I knocked on Dub's door. This was the first time that I had seen him at home all day. Normally he would sleep all day and out all night. It was going on midnight, and he hadn't been out of the house at all.

"Come in," he yelled from inside of his room. I slowly opened the door. He was laid back in the bed with nothing but some boxers on. He had his hands folded behind his back. He looked at me for a second and then looked back at the TV.

"So you gone tell me what that was about earlier," I quizzed. The whole time that were watching the movie all could think about was that damn kiss.

"What you mean?" he sat up. See he was playing games. He knew what the hell I meant. I leaned against the dresser before speaking.

"You kissed me out the blue Dub. What's up with that. You got me confused and shit. One minute you want to take me on dates and spend time then I look up and you acting like I don't exist," I told him. Dub had his days.

"Look Allia. A nigga feeling you. I don't want to be your friend. I want to be your man. Every time that we talk you want to make it seem like I'm your friend and shit. I ain't with that," he gritted. I let what he said sink in. He was telling me that he was ready to be with me. Honestly, I had been waiting to hear that.

"Dub, look, you need to know that I can't take another broken heart. I know that you have a million females. I just can't share so if I have to share then we can leave shit how it is," I told him. He got off the bed and made his way to me. His room was so big that it took him a second to get to me. When he did, he picked me up and kissed me, causing me to moan out.

"So you ready to mine?" he asked as he took me over to his bed. Before I knew it, he was pulling my shirt over my head. At that point, I had no control. He had my ass undressed so fast. Once I was undressed, he stood over me softly kissing on my body. I had been waiting on this shit for so damn long. There had been plenty of time that I just wanted to give it to him, but I knew that I was healing and I didn't want it to be a rebound love. I wanted it to be genuine.

"I asked you a question Allia." He was making his way to my center, and I was on edge. I damn near wanted to grab his head and put it where I needed it. I hate that shit. I was a get to the point type of person.

"Yes," I moaned praying that would make him get closer to where I needed him to be. When his lip touched my clit, I damn near died. Then I thought about the fact that if I died that I would miss out on this good ass head, I was about to get. When I said that he attacked my shit. I just laid there looking at the ceiling. I had been wanting this for the longest, and now that I was getting it I was stuck.

"Damn baby you taste just like I thought you would," he said as he licked my clit. "Can I make that pussy cum?"

I nodded my head because I couldn't talk. He knew that shit when he asked me. For the rest of the night, we made love. It was by far the best sex that I had ever had in my life.

38

DAEJA

I knew that my ears had to have been deceiving me. I just knew that Allia and my brother were not having sex. She was loud as if they were the only ones on the damn house. I got out of bed, grabbed my Air Pods and stuck them in my ears. I didn't want to hear that shit. I found my favorite playlist before grabbing my books so that I could study. I had a test coming up, and I needed to ace it so that my GPA wouldn't drop. I was almost done with school, and there was no way that I was going to let that happen. By the time that I was done studying it was three in the morning. I closed my book and laid back in my bed. Soon as my eye closed my text notification went off.

Gram: wyd: Me: nothing just laying here. Wyd

Gram: same what you got planned when you get up

Why was he asking me that? He never wanted to know what I was doing. I just laid there trying to think about if I wanted to tell him what I had going. I planned to kick it with Sam since it had been a while. After all the shit had happened in the past month, or so I just needed time alone. I knew that she was not going to give me space. Sam was nosey and jealous as hell. She always wanted to know what was going on in my life.

Me: nothing really whats up

I wish that he would ask me out, but he was too damn worried about my brothers. I knew that he was Dub's best friend, but damn I needed love too. I needed to know that I was good enough. I probably shouldn't have been thinking about messing with anyone, but I think a part of me needed to know that I could be loved. I wanted someone that would be in my life because they wanted to be and not for personal gain. I was so in my thoughts that I had drifted off to sleep. I was awakened by my damn phone ring back to back. I looked to see that it was Sam calling me. I needed to get up, so I didn't answer. I got up and headed to take care of my hygiene. Once I was done with that grabbed my phone so that I could call her back.

"Bitch I been calling yo ass all morning," she said soon as she answered the phone. It was only nine so what the hell did she mean by calling all morning. I hadn't really been talking to her.

"I was sleep you know that's what people do in the mornings, but what's up," I said trying my best not to have an attitude.

"Are we still meeting or what?"

"I told you that I was meeting you this evening and yo ass calling me at nine in the morning?" I asked for clarification.

"Damn bitch just call me when you ready cause yo attitude on ten this morning," she said before hanging up. I just threw the phone down. I really didn't feel like dealing with her ass. I got up and headed to see what my nasty ass brother and friend was doing. I walked in the kitchen, and they both were sitting at the island making googly eyes at each other and shit.

"Nasty asses," I mumbled as I walked past them. They both looked at me and busted out laughing. I didn't see shit funny. I looked at Dub, and he shrugged his shoulders as if he didn't do shit wrong. I rolled my eye before grabbing a piece of bacon.

"Aw so you can eat my food, but you called me nasty," Allia said licking her tongue out. As much as I wanted to be mad, I couldn't because they were so cute together. It had been years since I had seen Dub smile like this. In all honesty, I think that they are meant for each other. I'm just happy that she was my friend before they met. I knew that she was a true friend and that she would never fold on me or my family.

"Shut up," I said walking out the kitchen. On the way to my room, I scrolled Facebook and Instagram. I hadn't posted in a while because of everything that was going on. As long as Corry ass was still walking around, I wasn't going to post. He had been all in my inbox, but I hadn't been opening the messages. I just wanted him to leave me alone. Hell, he was the reason my ass couldn't sleep most nights. I will never forget the things that they did to me in that house. I was embarrassed to even talk about them. That was something that I wanted to forget about. Since it was still early, I set my alarm and got back in the bed. I wanted to get some more sleep.

"Dub I'm headed to go and meet Sam," I yelled to my brother from the hallway. I wanted to leave before his ass came in asking a million damn questions. I knew that I didn't need to be meeting her, but I needed to know why she did me so dirty. That shit was foul, and I didn't want to address it on the phone. I had even told my brothers that I knew she had something to do with it.

"Where you meeting her at?" he asked just as I walked out the door.

"Houston's," I advised. I knew that he needed to know my every location, but I was about tired of it. I need space.

"Ok be careful and if you feel some shit ain't right call me," he said before kissing me and walking back towards his office. That was way too damn easy. That only meant that someone was going to be watching me. I locked up then headed to my car.

Me: I'm finna go and meet Sam. Just letting you know

Gram: ok

I pulled out of the driveway and headed to my destination. When I pulled up in the lot, there were a lot of cars. The lot was packed. I called her to see where she was parked, but she didn't answer. I sat in my car for a minute then decide just to go inside. When I walked in the door, I went straight to the restroom. Just as I was about to walk in something caught my attention. I had to do a double take to make sure that I wasn't seeing shit. I walked a little closer but made sure that I was out of sight. Sam was standing in the corner talking to Corry.

I pulled out my phone so that I could snap a picture. Soon as I did, I sent it to Gram.

Gram: walk back to the door

I didn't as I was told. I swear I was doing my best to hide the fact that I was shaking. How could Sam do this to me? She was supposed to be my friend. She knew all the pain that he had caused me. When I made it to the door Gram was there. He held me tight before walking me back outside. We sat in his car until they walked out the door together. She had called me damn near twenty times. She was seriously setting me up that was some shit that I just couldn't wrap my mind around. This was someone that I thought was my friend. They walk around the side of the build. I knew that would be the last time that I saw them because Gram had some people waiting for them. Once the guy told Gram that they had them we walked to my car. He let the guy that was with him drive his. I was too shaken up.

The whole way to my house I cried. I was hurt and disappointed. At least I knew now shit was going to be a lot better.

39

GRAM

I needed to go ahead and tell Dub what was up with Daeja and me. For the past few weeks, we had been texting back and forth. I wanted to be with her, and the only way that could happen was if I got the ok from Dub and Jabo. I had my nigga to take both Sam and the Corry nigga to the warehouse. I was headed to take her home so that I could talk to them then we were going to kill these motherfuckers. I wish that Daeja would have listened all the times that we told her that Sam was not her friend. That bitch had been sneaky from the jump.

"You ok? I asked as we pulled in their driveway.

"Yea I'm ok as long as I'm with you," she assured me causing me to blush. She was the only female that had that effect on me. When I parked I pulled out my phone to find out where my nigga was that was driving my car since we were in hers. He told me that he was pulling in to Grip's shop. I had him drop it there because I didn't want him knowing where Dub lived. He was cool just not that damn cool.

"Look we have to tell Dub because I can't keep doing this. I'm a grown ass man, and I don't do the sneaking shit."

"Ok," was all that she said. I could look in her face and see that she was scared, but there was no need to be. I helped her out the car, and we walked in the door together. I didn't tell Dub what had happened. I just told him that I was one the way with her.

"You ok?" he asked he soon as he laid eyes on her. She nodded her head, and then sat on the couch beside Allia. I could see the worry in his eyes, but he didn't need to worry because she was ok. I was going to always make sure of that.

"Aye let's talk in the kitchen," I requested. Dub and Jabo both followed behind me. I looked at them both, and they both had a worried look on their face. I knew there was a chance that they were going to be mad, but I was will to take that chance for Daeja.

"What's up?" Dub asked. I sighed before looking at them.

"Look I need to tell yall some shit. I'm in love with Daeja. She feels the same. I can see the look on yall face. We haven't had sex or no shit like that, but I want to be the one to make her happy," I explained. They both just looked at me. I was waiting for them to say something, but neither of them did.

Dub walked off and went to sit at the table. Jabo just shook his head. "We were wondering when you were going to tell us," Dub said shocking me.

"Nigga you could have thought that we didn't notice how you managed to be around so much and the fact that you hadn't been talking to any hoes. Let's not forget the googly eyes shit yall be on," Jabo added. I just shook my head. I should have known that they noticed. I just laughed. I couldn't wait to tell Daeja this shit.

"Look she's grown, and we know that you will treat her right. Just keep her happy," Jabo said hugging me. Dub got up and did the same. I was happy that this shit was over with because I was tired of sneaking around.

"In other business, I got something for yall at the warehouse," I told then causing them to smile.

"Sounds like music to my ears. Oh and you gotta tell Pops on yo own," Dub laughed. I didn't even think about his ass. We all walked to the front to see the girls chatting. I knew that they already knew. We all chilled until it got dark then we headed to end our problems. All three of us piled in Dub's Range and headed to the warehouse. On the ride there we got a call saying that some had spotted the Slim nigga. He was the last loose string since they had killed Cell. That nigga body was found the other day in an alley.

"Let's get this shit done so that we can take care of the Slim nigga and get back home," I said as we got out the car. They both nodded as we made our way to the back of the warehouse.

"Dub, please help me," Sam cried soon as we walked in. Dub just laughed. Deaja had told us that she was the one that set her up with the Corry nigga.

"I'ma help you like you helped my sister," Dub said sending a bullet through her head. I just knew that he was going to torture her ass. I guess he was ready to get back home just like I was. I shrugged and let off my whole clip off into Corry's chest.

"Clean this shit up," was all Jabo said before walking off. Me and Dub followed behind him. We jumped back in the truck and headed to the next destination. The Slim nigga was dumber than we thought he was still living at the house that they were holding Daeja at. The ride out there was long, but it was well worth it. When we pulled up the nigga was getting out of his car. Jabo sent a bullet through his head before he had a chance to run.

"Mission Complete," Jabo said as we turned around and walked back to the car. Soon as Dub started the car, I lit blunt. Life was now on track.

40

ALLIA

A YEAR LATER

"Bae you know that you don't need to be picking that shit up," Dub fussed at me. We were getting things together for Jacey's sixth birthday party. I was picking up a box that held the candy bags. The box was light as hell.

"Dub I'm good. I'm pregnant, not handicapped," I fussed back. Yes, you heard me right I had let Dub knock my ass up.

"As long as you are pregnant with my son you handicapped, now give me this damn box," he demanded, I just rolled my eyes and handed it to him. He was so extra. I followed him to the back yard where I was headed until his ass stopped me. Once he sat the box down, I started to pull the bags out the box. Dub was on the other side of the yard helping the guy with the bounce house. Life was so good for me. I wouldn't have ever thought that run-in into someone's car would bring me so much happiness. With Dub, I felt complete. He was the part of me that was missing.

"Allia can I eat this now?" Jacey asked. She was holding a cupcake from the table in the house that she was not supposed to touch. Jacey was my baby. She had been here with us for the past year. We hadn't heard from her mother not once. Word on the street was that she was on drugs bad.

"Yes, baby." She knew that I wasn't going to tell her no especially not today. It was her day so she could do what she wanted. Once I was done with the treat table, I wobbled my way back in the house.

"Can yall get a room?" I joked as I watched Gram and Daeja all hugged up. They were inseparable. If you saw Gram, you saw Dae. They were so cute together. Daeja was set to graduate from college in a few months. Gram had finally opened a restaurant, and it was doing good.

"Find you some business," Deaja joked. I just shook my head and went to get the balloons from the garage. I was waiting on Erin's ass to come over. She said that she was on the way hours ago. Her and Jabo had just come back from their honeymoon. They couldn't be like normal people and take a week they ass had been gone for a damn month. I picked my phone up to call her ass. She knew that I needed her.

"Damn I'm on the way," she answered.

"Bitch you live next door there is no way that it should take that damn long," I told her ass. I knew that they nasty ass was probably over there fucking as always. She could use the kids as an excuse because they were with his mother. Erin was now a wife and mother of two. She had their daughter JoyceLynn five months ago. She was the cutest baby ever and spitting image of her father. They got married a few months before she had JoyceLynn. They were both doing good. She was in school to be a doctor like her father although Jabo didn't want her working.

"I'm walking in the door," she said before hanging up. I knew that she was mad because I had called her again, but I didn't care. A few minutes later she walked in the house blushing with Jabo right behind her.

I guess you could say that life was good for all of us. We all were happy and in love. I guess that's what happens when you get Wifed up by a Memphis Hustla.

The End

TEXTING LIST

To stay up to date on new releases, plus get exclusive information on contests, sneak peeks, and more...

Text ColeHartSig to (855)231-5230